The Collected Sonnets
of William Shakespeare,
Zombie

CONTRIBUTIONS TO ZOMBIE STUDIES

White Zombie: *Anatomy of a Horror Film*. Gary D. Rhodes. 2001

The Zombie Movie Encyclopedia. Peter Dendle. 2001

American Zombie Gothic: The Rise and Fall (and Rise) of the Walking Dead in Popular Culture. Kyle William Bishop. 2010

Back from the Dead: Remakes of the Romero Zombie Films as Markers of Their Times. Kevin J. Wetmore, Jr. 2011

Generation Zombie: Essays on the Living Dead in Modern Culture. Edited by Stephanie Boluk and Wylie Lenz. 2011

Race, Oppression and the Zombie: Essays on Cross-Cultural Appropriations of the Caribbean Tradition. Edited by Christopher M. Moreman and Cory James Rushton. 2011

Zombies Are Us: Essays on the Humanity of the Walking Dead. Edited by Christopher M. Moreman and Cory James Rushton. 2011

The Zombie Movie Encyclopedia, Volume 2: 2000–2010. Peter Dendle. 2012

Great Zombies in History. Edited by Joe Sergi. 2013 (graphic novel)

Unraveling Resident Evil: *Essays on the Complex Universe of the Games and Films*. Edited by Nadine Farghaly. 2014

"We're All Infected": Essays on AMC's The Walking Dead *and the Fate of the Human*. Edited by Dawn Keetley. 2014

Zombies and Sexuality: Essays on Desire and the Living Dead. Edited by Shaka McGlotten and Steve Jones. 2014

...But If a Zombie Apocalypse Did *Occur: Essays on Medical, Military, Governmental, Ethical, Economic and Other Implications*. Edited by Amy L. Thompson and Antonio S. Thompson. 2015

How Zombies Conquered Popular Culture: The Multifarious Walking Dead in the 21st Century. Kyle William Bishop. 2015

Zombifying a Nation: Race, Gender and the Haitian Loas on Screen. Toni Pressley-Sanon. 2016

Living with Zombies: Society in Apocalypse in Film, Literature and Other Media. Chase Pielak and Alexander H. Cohen. 2017

Romancing the Zombie: Essays on the Undead as Significant "Other." Edited by Ashley Szanter and Jessica K. Richards. 2017

The Written Dead: Essays on the Literary Zombie. Edited by Kyle William Bishop and Angela Tenga. 2017

The Collected Sonnets of William Shakespeare, Zombie. William Shakespeare and Chase Pielak. 2018

Dharma of the Dead: Zombies, Mortality and Buddhist Philosophy. Christopher M. Moreman. 2018

The Subversive Zombie: Social Protest and Gender in Undead Cinema and Television. Elizabeth Aiossa. 2018

The Collected Sonnets of William Shakespeare, Zombie

WILLIAM SHAKESPEARE
and CHASE PIELAK

CONTRIBUTIONS TO ZOMBIE STUDIES
Series Editor, Kyle William Bishop

McFarland & Company, Inc., Publishers
Jefferson, North Carolina

ALSO OF INTEREST BY WILLIAM SHAKESPEARE FROM MCFARLAND (EDITED BY DEMITRA PAPADINIS): *The Tragedie of Macbeth: A Frankly Annotated First Folio Edition* (2012); *As You Like It: A Frankly Annotated First Folio Edition* (2011); *The Tragedie of Romeo and Juliet: A Frankly Annotated First Folio Edition* (2010)

All illustrations are by Anna Pagnucci

LIBRARY OF CONGRESS CATALOGUING-IN-PUBLICATION DATA

Names: Pielak, Chase, 1981– author. | Shakespeare, William, 1564–1616. Sonnets.
Title: The collected sonnets of William Shakespeare, zombie / William Shakespeare and Chase Pielak.
Description: Jefferson, North Carolina : McFarland & Company, Inc., Publishers, 2018. | Series: Contributions to zombie studies | Includes index.
Identifiers: LCCN 2018004404 | ISBN 9781476671154 (softcover : acid free paper) ∞
Subjects: LCSH: Shakespeare, William, 1564–1616—Parodies, imitations, etc. | Zombies—Poetry. | Humorous poetry.
Classification: LCC PS3616.I336 C65 2018 | DDC 811/.6—dc23
LC record available at https://lccn.loc.gov/2018004404

BRITISH LIBRARY CATALOGUING DATA ARE AVAILABLE

ISBN (print) 978-1-4766-7115-4
ISBN (ebook) 978-1-4766-3130-1

Front cover image of altered portrait of William Shakespeare © 2018 duncan1890/iStock

Printed in the United States of America

McFarland & Company, Inc., Publishers
Box 611, Jefferson, North Carolina 28640
www.mcfarlandpub.com

Acknowledgments

I will walk eternally grateful to Lori Anne Ferrell for opening my eyes to Shakespeare's world. Alaina Pascarella heard my first groans. Katherine Bishop gave me hope that the dead might rise. Isaiah, Kira, Nathaniel, and Isaac; Katherine; and Aidan, Sara, and Sam have become my horde.

Anna Pagnucci's visions lend beauty to the apocalypse. Thank you.

Table of Contents

CXXX

My mistress' eyes are nothing like the sun;
Coral is far more red, than her lips red:
If snow is white, why then her breasts are wan;
If hairs are wires, black wires plaster her head.
I have seen roses damasked, red and white,
But no such roses see I in her cheeks;
And in most perfumes is there more delight
Than in the breath that from my mistress reeks.
I love to hear her groan, yet well I know
That music has a far more pleasing sound:
I grant I never saw a goddess go,—
My mistress, when she walks, shambles on the ground:
And yet by heaven, I think my love as rare,
As any Z belied with false compare.

Preface: Why Shakespeare and Zombies?

Sacrilege! How could I debase the most hallowed writer in the English language? How in heaven's name could a writer disrespect all that is holy in English literature? And oh good gracious, it's ridiculous to make this all seem plausible. Zombies are not real.

But what if they were? Fiction invites readers to look forward in time, to look back in time, and sometimes to imagine a parallel world that is contemporary but somehow unlike this one. It delights in the question, "what if?" What if there really were zombies? How might we react? How would the world be different if zombies existed? What if they existed in the past?

The beauty of fiction is that through its various impossible possibilities, we imagine the things of this world as otherworldy, and we can then face them head on. There is an ongoing conversation in academic circles about the nature of zombies. Among other things, they represent our fears of voicelessness, powerlessness, and dis-ease about living with each other. Zombies reflect historical and contemporary conditions of slavery and oppression. They represent grave fears of control and the loss of life. And yet, just as significantly, they are fun. They provide a release and an opportunity to suspend disbelief. Zombies populate popular film and television offering graphic gory images of our world, as if they roamed the earth.

Fiction allows us to explore questions that might otherwise be too daunting to handle. Here, it engages questions like: What does it mean to be a human being? What is my deepest fear? How would I respond if my child were to have passed in early youth, as Shakespeare's son,

1

Hamnet, did? What if the one I loved were to die? How would I react to fame? Could I resist myriad potential partners offering themselves to me? What would it be like to be someone with a different gender identity or sexual preference? What does it really mean to love someone? What does it mean to grow old and to watch my own face change? What if my lover's face aged? What if I were to die? These questions are all coded into Shakespeare's works already. This book reveals them by applying a zombie lens.

Language is slippery and playful. Poetry exposes, through form, gaps in the meaning of language. It forces readers to bring in their own worlds to fill in the gaps left by the spare words. We must make meaning from poetry even more obviously than prose fiction. Our interpretation reveals us to ourselves, as we interact with and make meaning from texts. At least it should. Through poetic fiction we can, perhaps, together explore these deepest of human impulses, uncertainties, and persistent certainties. I have endeavored to change the sonnets into zonnets by using as few alterations as possible in virtually every case. Even with only a few words' difference, or even a few letters' update, the sonnets succumb to plague quite readily. Shakespeare's own life, shrouded partially in mystery due to an apparent lack of interest in record keeping, remains somewhat obscure. So we will fill gaps with imagined extensions of ourselves, always exposing, revealing, opening.

The bits that have been modernized represent nothing more than an attempt to account for some of the language change of the last 400 years toward simplicity. There are, perhaps with all fiction, two slices of reality here carefully blended with illusion. Shakespeare was real and the details contained herein often closely mirror real events. His world and ours clash into a tidal wave of reality. The carefully introduced zombie stream, though fictive, represents an illusive veneer. The language modernization invites those less familiar with early modern English to engage the same questions.

In some ways the key question of the zombie inquires about what we might do if all social bets were off. If there were zombies, how would we live with each other, perhaps even how would we live at all? When Charles Lamb wrote in his essay "That We Should Rise with the Lark" that "we are already half acquainted with ghosts. We were never much in the world," he was ever only partially right. We live in the story that we tell ourselves. Every book that we read expands the bounds of our personal history.

So what do I hope for from you? For just a moment, I want you to say alongside C. S. Lewis and Walt Whitman before him that you have become a thousand others and yet remained yourself. I want you to see the night sky 400 years ago with the eyes of an Elizabethan even as you open them to the sunset of this day. I want you to transcend yourself and to become yourself in the same moment (*An Experiment in Criticism*). I want to offer you an escape into a world in which not only are zombies real, but in which they also populate our finest literature. I want you to be surprised at the facility with which the sonnets can be adapted to include zombies. Shakespeare's questions somehow seem so very near to our own. His fears are ours. His joys ours. The presence of a raging horde exposes, rather than vast differences in time and space and worldview, incredible similarities. And I want you to explore these persistent questions deeply embedded in human existence about love and voice and fears safely and without even realizing it—at first.

It is as true that zombies are real, in that if you were to see one you would recognize it, as it is at that they are not real, in the sense that you will not go outside your reading room and find one waiting to eat your brains. Yet this imaginative exploration, that is purely a work of fiction, and hopefully fun, nevertheless investigates deep questions about being and humanity as purposefully as any academic work. This book imagines the world as if zombies did exist already, inviting you to imagine alongside.

Origin Story
of the Zonnets

Good friend for Jesus sake forbeare,
To digg the dust encloased heare.
Bleste be the man that spares thes stones,
And curst be he that moves my bones.
—Shakespeare's Epitaph

After his closed-casket funeral on 25 April 1616, William Shakespeare's corpse was buried in his parish-church-floor deep under the epitaph inscribed above. He wrote the text before his burial, a posthumous joke. Few who live appreciate the biting humor and hard partying Shakespeare enjoyed during his last years. According to John Ward, who witnessed Shakespeare's final days, "Shakespeare, Drayton, and Ben Jonson had a merry meeting and it seems drank too hard, for Shakespeare died of a fever there contracted." The exact nature of Shakespeare's death, however, is never recorded. Neither is the nature of his fever. Fevers were still mystifying in the early 1600s. They were often attributed to some combination of bodily imbalance and bad air. And yet it is obvious that the link between drinking and fever covers some more insidious truth. This book records the real story of Shakespeare's end, including the long, slow descent toward becoming zombie. Fortunately for us, while he was losing his grip on humanity—in his most lucid moments—he kept writing. His real final writings are these: the zonnets.

Histories of the playwright often fail to address his sonnets, which were first published in 1609 by Thomas Thorpe. Unfortunately, the author never intended them to be published. The manuscript bears no authorization. Far more dishonestly, the sonnets were not published as they were written. Long before they were published, and long before his corpse was confined to the church floor, Shakespeare was bitten. These sonnets are restored to all their Technicolor and horrifying glory. They each struggle with becoming zombie.

The nature of the bite remains a matter of conjecture. The progression of the disease is similarly shrouded in mystery. Yet we do know that it was long before the mysterious fever Ford mentions. It seems very likely that the bite occurred on a dark evening in May 1598. This was a few years before the death of Queen Elizabeth I. On this night, in the midst of a raucous thunderstorm, Shakespeare had been out partying at the Tabard Inn with several of his contemporaries. The guests included his friends Michael Drayton and Ben Jonson. At some point in the evening, the revelry got so out of hand that the group was forced to leave, probably because they had taken to carving their names into the wall. When they left the inn, they walked the short distance up the bank of the Themes River to the Royal Menagerie at the Tower of London. After that night, and until the night of Shakespeare's supposed death, the crew was never seen together again.

The bite was the result of an encounter with a creature half fish and half human. While it is commonly assumed that Elizabeth's successor, James I, started the practice of animal fighting at the Tower, it probably began with the Queen. Bears, lions, and dogs fought to the death in the ring to the amazement of bloodthirsty spectators. The more exotic the animal, the more exciting the mayhem. On the fateful evening in question, the crowd was already hyped up to fever pitch by the vicious animal attacks within the ring.

And then the unthinkable happened: a creature captured somewhere in North Africa was unleashed. It was a creature of rot. A misshapen knave, a thing of darkness. Among its notable features were the protruding lower jaw anchoring flesh-tearing teeth, scaly and decaying flesh, and long, gory nails. Now, perhaps the creature's long nails dug the bard's end as it reached up over the short fence. Or the creature may have escaped the ring before being put down. But the encounter was unmistakably horrifying.

The venom took effect almost immediately. At first the symptoms were mild. Stupor, reeling drunkenness. Shakespeare walked into a dream world that night. As the weeks went by and turned into months, the outbreak took hold of his body. Flesh dropped in small flakes. And then the hunger began. The expansiveness and sublime feeling simultaneously shrank and blew up his world. His work flourished initially. It was the most productive period in his life.

Then locals began to suffer. Shakespeare began to crave a new food. Actors offered themselves during the earliest months. They begged to be cast at any price. One pound of flesh was a tiny price, two pounds a well-worth-it investment.

The disease demanded more and more flesh. Only human cells quenched the hunger—for a time. Before long, it took brains. In order to stay human, the daily dose grew exponentially until nothing but the brain would satisfy. The brain it was that opened the experience of a new life. A new perspective. He fed on the words and thoughts of the victims conveniently stored in their memories. No one conceived of stopping him. His subjects were taken into his mind even as his plays told their stories. Beautiful, terrible, Shakespeare's bodies bleed for us. His desk became their altar.

Lady Rosalind Cephalie was his first victim. Her porcelain skin and dark features live in his sonnets unparalleled. Her identity is nowhere else recorded; she has been erased from the story of history entirely except for the shiny gloss of her blood contrasting the brightness of her humanity. On the street he became a butcher eyeing the choicest cuts. Back in his room, temporarily full, he recorded their own memories as epitaphs.

Piece by piece, bite by bite the world began to crumble around him. It took decades to fail completely. And yet there were always more bodies: to fill his plays' audiences as groundlings and to sate his ravenous stomach. Countless souls in the new city, desperate for work: each was happy enough just to feed her or his family. Or perhaps they were driven by the chance to be memorialized forever, like Lady Cephalie.

The short-lived creature that first infected his future was immediately destroyed. But it was too late. The damage was done. Shakespeare's visit was recorded in the guest log on May 3 of that same year. The creature was never mentioned again except in his plays. The exact progression of the disease remains a mystery. However, there are hints throughout Shakespeare's body of plays that the world was far more dangerous than we have been led to believe.

In *Hamlet*, in fact, one of Shakespeare's most beloved plays, we find clear evidence of his altered state. Probably the first play written following his infection (begun in 1599 and completed in 1601), themes of mental disease and infection, poison, and tragic death darken the landscape of thinly veiled London. Hamlet's famous question, "Why was he sent into England?" is answered by the play's clown in an often overlooked statement: "Why, because he was mad: he shall recover his wits there; or, if he do not, it's no great matter there." The madness slowly raging through England's streets is none other than the beginnings of apocalypse that had already partially claimed a most famous victim.

Ophelia describes the looks of her former fiancé, Hamlet "as if he had been loosed out of hell / to speak of horrors." And it is no accident that Guildenstern's character suggests that there has been "much throwing about of brains." These lines have always been read metaphorically because scholars and actors alike failed to recognize Shakespeare's condition. Now, their importance is felt.

Most official chronologies agree that Shakespeare's plays were all complete by 1613, and all of the late plays bear the mark of other hands than those of the bard. The time between the wild night with Jonson and Drayton and the publication of the altered sonnets in 1609 carves out the last aware period of Shakespeare's life. The details of the flowing years are simply too dramatic and the alteration too horrifying to survive in contemporary accounts. His last few years of relative unproductivity are quite explained by his far deteriorated condition.

Returning to the epitaph over his grave, the reason for the curse on those who would dig his grave is ever too obvious in this light. Shakespeare's zombie corpse is trapped in his tomb. The wandering carrion had become too dangerous to allow it to haunt the streets and the cover-up began. During the beginning of this long period, following infection and ending with his undead confinement, Shakespeare continued to write zombie infected sonnets that reflected the real conditions of his locale, bustling London.

William Shakespeare was not otherwise alone in the world. He married when he was 18 years old and had three children with Anne Hathaway. With various strands of plague circulating through the country, it was too dangerous for Anne to reunite with her husband after his move to the London theater district. Anne remained behind in Stratford. Several of his zonnets wistfully admire his separated love.

In the meantime, Anne had born him three children, Susanna, Hamnet, and Judith. Tragically, Hamnet died in 1596 at age 11, in what has often been described as an outbreak of the bubonic plague. It is tempting, of course, to speculate that this was connected to his father's zombiefication.

As soon as his daughter Susanna was married, the already wealthy and by then quite-infected Shakespeare changed his will to name her as executor, leaving her most of his property. This was still nearly a decade before his death. The playwright was desperate to secure the success of his family before completing the turn. Perhaps the most heartbreaking sign of disease begins in 1608. That was the year that his granddaughter, Elizabeth, was born. Shakespeare was never allowed to see his granddaughter because of the danger of infection.

Shakespeare's loves, fears, heartbreaks, and hope for the future make their way into each of these zonnets. Even the contradictions that plagued his mind rear up here. Each of the 154 sonnets contained herein records the life of one specific, irreplaceable victim, or one moment of his own life given over to the disease. They are dedicated to the moment of experience held in the victim's brain just at the end. The very last memory. Each is immediately human. Each epitaph represents the coming together of Shakespeare and his food. These poems are prayers of thanks for the sacrifices, even as they remember the living victim. The zonnets treat several distinct themes: apocalyptic beauty, hunger, increase, life's better condition as a zombie, time, apocalyptic living, the profoundly hopeful possibility of zombabies, surviving the apocalypse, the desire to prevent death, epitaphs, the horde, grave love, cures, and the inevitability of falling apart. Each theme is organized into a chapter, though there is considerable overlap. The reader will find a key to cross-reference the restored zonnet to its 1609 number at the end of the book.

This is the book of sonnets Shakespeare would have authorized if he had been spared the disgrace of undead burial for only a few more months. The horror of torn flesh rarely intrudes; rather the poet's horror at his own drifting humanity is almost always tangible. He was grateful for each one. And mortified at his own hunger. Even so, it drove him onward.

It is perhaps worth noting, finally, that it is uncertain whether or not a cure was ever developed. If we take into account the recent popularity of zombie films and books, there must be some truth to the rumors that these creatures existed. If a cure was found, it is now lost. Zombies have again begun to walk the earth. The minor outbreaks have all been quickly squashed by overzealous governments too eager to prevent their citizens from learning the truth and unleashing the kind of world-destroying panic that will inevitably bring about the end of humanity.

So savor the wit and wisdom that course through each of these tiny poems. They prove that life wasn't always as it is now; it was always more terrifying, more tasty, and more tumultuous.

Shakespeare's Undead Introduction: Life Is Better Now

> *O, that this too, too sullied flesh would melt,*
> *Thaw, and resolve itself into a dew,*
> *How weary, stale, flat, and unprofitable*
> *Seem to me all the uses of this world!*
> *Fie on 't, ah fie! 'Tis an unweeded garden*
> *That grows to seed. Things rank and gross in nature*
> *Possess it merely. That it should come to this*
> *But two months dead nay, not so much, not two....*
> —Hamlet, *Hamlet* (I.2)

Life is better now. The rotten stink of London's cesspool streets has gone with my sense of smell. Wandering rank things always possessed the world, but now they have the courage to show what they wear inside. And yet, dearest love, that you remain with me even now, wandering in undeath, gives me strength to shamble on. Though we're clothed in ragged weeds, we have no care in the world. Though flesh falls from our faces, our mouths still have lips to touch, and tongues to taste, and teeth to tear.

Every day now is a study in contradiction. My attitude must be forever inconstant and ambiguous; it is I who am torn. I look upon your face, no longer blushing, and my soul cries out. It has been three scant years since that frightful day, when the festering wound on your arm took you. And yet the world only gets brighter now. We will be forever together, now, my Juliet. With each passing cloud, each ticking second, I see more of your heart. Food is plentiful. You no longer have

13

to struggle to find yourself. And my muse has never so freely granted my pen ink. We have no need to wait to act, to carefully consider, to wonder if you love or not. No blushes mar your complexion. Not anymore. Every groan is sincere. Every green given by nature. I wake in the morning content and hungry. I pause during dreamless night, never tormented by thoughts of growing old or looming death. I am tormented by the very perfection of decay.

Ophelia, Cordelia, Lavinia, and my lovely Juliet wander freely, returned from their graves. But, dear reader, Elizabeth wears the crown. Always made up in life, she still wears the painted plaster from the funeral. Even without the brocade gown, she would be the most regal of us, shaming the dawn for splendor. She leads her horde with ever and unnatural prowess; it is the envy of other nations; she leads our country again without parallel in the world. The queen is dead, long live the queen! And we are one with her, alongside her, her equals each.

And yet! Every human remains an opportunity to grow the beauty of the horde. Help me, my cupid, spear them with our mouth's arrows to set them free to love as we do. Let us make them merry to the point of death; plant his pale flag on their faces and open their eyes to our joy. And though their brains may become as dry as biscuits bitten by worms, our work is clear. Feed, my dear. Let us love the world.

1

Apocalyptic Beauty

"Decay itself is beautiful."
—John Ruskin, *Modern Painters*

"Could you lie and tell me that I'm still beautiful? That I'm still your muse?" she asked that fateful morning. Dawn had just broken through the attic window and rays of sun molded tangible around her skin. Its pallor shone opalescent. "No lie needed, Juliet. You are the sun."

She reached for me from across an impossible cleft—as if I wasn't already there next to her. I never left. For the span of a night her vacant stare opened toward the stars. And then she was back—or some part of her was back. Was it the best or worst?

Still. It is the perfect word for apocalyptic beauty. Static and unchanged. Unmoving. Frozen in time and at peace with the entirety of the world. Undoubtedly as radiant as the moon, still. Still magnetic. Possessed of a heart that is, still, still. Now come to terms with the world as it is. Isn't there something better when we see the world for what it is, see the lives of the people in it as shams, upheld for the consumption of others, really only quite as shambling as our own? The illusion that even Elizabeth or her Robert might have it all together is as false as wooden teeth. But finding the good in the world anyway: that is the secret of apocalyptic beauty. When beauty continues in the face of the broken, or better—when it shines through because of the cracks, that is apocalyptic beauty. Sometime after trying to get as far away as possible, when we've given in to the desperate desire to escape and returned, there is comfort. There is beauty.

So on that day, after she'd eaten of the tree of the knowledge of

good and evil, after becoming mine, she awoke to the world that no longer fears to hide its beauty. It is a simpler world, sadder, and full of contradictions. It is pearl-poisoned wine and candied pears. It is the swan in flight against a tempest. Nevertheless, it bleeds forth its alloyed loveliness to all those who care to look.

As is evident, despite apparent inarticulacy, we still speak. Our words that have fallen so silent since still ring through the shroud. Groans you've heard. Sure. Yet it's the whisperings that betray the secret. The still small longings of the heart do not die in passing. The hopes and fears that plagued life alter before the plague. They do not, however, disappear. Insecurity haunts even the undead. Fear of the eternal—not of the apocalypse—but of the accounting to come after weighs. But for most moments, fearlessness is the order of the day. Despite whatever lingering doubts persist, craving crushes will. Soaring moments of the soul that satisfy aesthetic longing live on, the bastard children of the apocalypse. Perhaps I am an unreliable storyteller.

Reader, surely you don't believe me. You couldn't. It has been years since the plague hit the streets and since my muse had been bitten. The flesh around the wound had long since ceased to cling. It wasn't alone; her smile alternately drooped and flashed, baring teeth or closed. And even so, she looked almost as fresh as the day I'd met her—to me. She'd willingly offered her arm that day, the one now so bare. I can practically still taste the blush skin. Even then I couldn't walk through the streets without being thronged. Poor girls had nothing—no food, no jobs, no hope. And boys. I was their only way out. It was enough to offer a chance at existing, no matter how poor its quality. A lottery of flesh. The line for a ticket stretched around the block at the theater. One bite from me and they were set. Prime rib was always my favorite.

Of course, I offered something else, too. Something far better. It is in these verses that my real gift lay. These rigid numbers held tenuously the gift of eternal life—free from rot—coffined or otherwise. They were the only way to survive. This remains the only way to escape the rot. Yet even so, rife decay formed a new object of beauty. Apocalyptic beauty.

It's funny. Exceedingly fair skin had always been de rigueur. How much more so now? Cosmetics, rather than expiring in their due time, are even more important. Those still alive will, as often as not, imitate the cooling spread of infection. Rosy dawn has been supplanted by gray dusk. All after the Queen, of course. Gloriana! Plaster, pale, dusted with a hint of sooten ash, dyes the skin. Even those most recently succumbed, those still bearing the first blush of the grave, douse themselves, obscuring canker. Tinctures of fresh thyme rubbed violently over the cheeks, forehead, and chest lend verdure to the otherwise dull.

Bright star-eyes shining from heaven don't matter a lick anymore. Except as appetizers. And still we can see. Flat, pale, pallid. The irony of zombie sight is that though eyes look cataract-covered, they're just as clear as they were in life. The tiniest speck remains as invisible as it ever was. It's the other senses that compensate, though. Suddenly, I can hear everything. Hoards moaning for miles up the Themes ring out loud and clear. Every victim's screams of anguish echo in my skull, a symphonic testimony sweeter than the songs of William Byrd. And he was a delicious swan if I've ever tasted one.

But that's nothing compared to the olfactory improvements that come part and parcel with the plague. Every whiff of living flesh arises, a sweet scent toward heaven, caught along the way. Masterful chefs could not have begun to approach the natural artistry of the scent of raw brains. Sumptuary laws be damned, too. Fish on Wednesday, Friday, and Saturday has blissfully given way to the most artful combinations of flesh displayed, tooth-sashimi style. Every tidbit has a place, arranged, undecayed.

If there is anything beautiful, it is fresh flesh, new reared. A million shadows disperse darkness around the beauteous. The light of death shines forth, decay reigns. Beautiful words stand testimony to the continuation of beauty, picturesque, in the everyday. The most wondrous remnant persistent is surely grace. In her, her lilt, of body and jaw, it lives. In his brow, forlorn in the face of threnody, beauty lives.

XCIX

The forward skunkweed thus did I chide:
Sweet thief, from where did you steal your odor
If not from my love's breath? The purple veins
Which on your soft belly contrast abide
In my love's veins you have too grossly dyed.

The lily I condemned for your hand,
Buds of marjoram still have stolen your hair;
The roses fearfully on thorns did stand,
One blushing shame, another white despair;
A third, not red nor white, had stolen of both,
And to his robbery had annexed your breath;
But, despite their thefts, and pride of all growth
A vengeful canker ate you up to death.
More flowers I noted, yet none I could see,
Without features robbed from your past plenty.

LIV

O! how much more does beauty beauteous seem
By that sweet ornament which death does give.
The rose looks fair, but fairer we it deem
For that sweet odor, which does in it live.
The canker blooms have full as deep a dye
As the perfumed tincture of the roses.
Hang on such thorns, and play as wantonly
When summer's breath their masked buds discloses:
But, for their virtue only is their show,
They live unwood, and unrespected fade;
Die to themselves. Sweet roses do not so;
Of their sweet deaths, are sweetest odors made:
And so of you, beauteous and living friend,
When voice shall cease, my verse distills your end.

LXXXIII

Still not once have I seen you painting need,
And therefore to gray hue no painting set;
I found, or thought I found, you did exceed
That barren tender of a poet's debt:
And therefore I have rested in your court
That your law, being extant, so rightly shows

How far all words must come too short;
Speaking of worth, what worth in your spring grows.
Quiet sentence for my sin imputed,
You shall be my glory though I am dumb;
For I don't impair beauty being muted,
While others would try life, and bring a tomb.
There remains more life in one of your eyes
Than all your poets can in praise devise.

XX

A woman's face with virus' own hand painted,
Hast thou, the master mistress of my passion;
A beast's savage heart, and well acquainted
With shifting change, as is false women's fashion:
An eye more bright than theirs, less fixed but rolling,
Gazing the object whereupon it grazes;
A man in hue all "hues" in his controlling,
Which steals men's eyes and women's souls amazes.
And for a woman were you first created;
Till Nature, as she wrought you, fell a-doting,
And by addition me of you defeated,
By adding one thing to your purpose: feeding.
But since your arm's pricked for nature's pleasure,
Mine be your love and your love's use my treasure.

LIII

What is your substance, whereof are you made,
That millions of strange shadows on you tend?
Since every one, has every one, one shade,
And you but one, can every shadow lend.
Deathly Adonis, false life's counterfeit
Is poorly imitated after you;
On Helen's cheek all art of beauty set,
And you in Grecian tears are painted new:

Speak of the spring, and foison of the year,
The one doth shadow of your beauty show,
The other as your bounty doth appear;
And you in every blessed shape we know.
In all external grace you have some part,
But you like none, none you, for constant heart.

IV

Unthrifty loveliness, why do you spend
Upon yourself your beauty's legacy?
Haven't you seen what happens in the end?
Yes, nature only lends to those are free:
Then, beauteous stinge, why do you abuse
The bounteous largess given you to give?
Profitless usurer, why do you use
So great a sum of sums, yet cannot live?
For having traffic with yourself alone,
You of your self your sweet self does deceive:
Then how when nature calls you to decease,
What acceptable audit can you leave?
Your unused molars must be tombed with you
Or turned monstrous, nothing but rot to rue.

LXVII

Ah! wherefore with infection should he live,
And with his presence grace society,
That death by him advantage should achieve,
And lace itself with his variety?
Why should false makeup imitate his cheek,
And steal dead seeming of his living hue?
Why should poor beauty indirectly seek
Roses of shadow, since his rose is true?
Why should he live, now Nature bankrupt is,
Robbed blind of blood to blush through lively veins?

For she hath no capital now but his,
And proud of many, lives upon his gains.
She deposits him to prove wealth she'd had
In days long gone, before these last so bad.

LXVIII

Thus is his cheek the map of days outworn,
When beauty lived and died as flowers do now,
Before these bastard undead beasts were born,
Or dared inhabit in a living brow;
Before the golden tresses of the dead,
The right of sepulchers, were shorn away,
To live a second life on second head;
Ere beauty's dead fleece made another gay:
In him those holy antique hours are seen,
Without all ornament, natural, true,
Making no summer of another's green,
Robbing no old to dress his beauty new;
And his genetic map Nature should store,
To show false Art what beauty was before.

LXII

Sin of self-love possesses all my eye
And all my soul, and all my every part;
And for this sin there is no remedy,
It is so grounded deep inside my heart.
I think no face is as gracious as mine,
No shape so true, no truth of such account;
And for myself my own worth does define,
As I all other in all worths surmount.
But when my mirror shows my face truly
Beaten and chopped with tanned antiquity,
My own self-love ridiculous I see;
Self so self-loving is iniquity.

Yet you, creature, supply my shape's contrast:
My visage whole, yours a gangrenous waste.

CXXVII

In the old age green was not counted fair,
Or if it were, it bore not beauty's name;
But now is rot beauty's successive heir,
And beauty slandered with a bastard shame:
For since each hand hath put on Nature's power,
Fairing the foul with Art's false borrowed face,
Sweet beauty hath no name, no holy bower,
But is profaned, if not lives in disgrace.
Therefore my mistress' eyes are snowy white,
Her eyes so suited, and they mourners seem
At such who, not reborn, fail beauty's sight,
Slandering recreation with false esteem:
Yet so they mourn becoming like their foe,
Yet every tongue says beauty will taste so.

CXXX

My mistress' eyes are nothing like the sun;
Coral is far more red, than her lips red:
If snow is white, why then her breasts are wan;
If hairs are wires, black wires plaster her head.
I have seen roses damasked, red and white,
But no such roses see I in her cheeks;
And in most perfumes is there more delight
Than in the breath that from my mistress reeks.
I love to hear her groan, yet well I know
That music has a far more pleasing sound:
I grant I never saw a goddess go,—
My mistress, when she walks, shambles on the ground:
And yet by heaven, I think my love as rare,
As any Z belied with false compare.

2

Hunger

Why, there they are, both baked in this pie,
Whereof their mother daintily hath fed,
Eating the flesh that she herself hath bred.
—*Titus*, Titus Andronicus (V.3)

The first rule of the apocalypse is simple: feed. The taste of brains is so much more beautiful than food had been. Can food really be beautiful, you ask? Yes, reader. Yes. There is no taste like the taste of fresh flesh. The flesh of kin tastes so familiar and warm. It reminds me of the holiday feast, shared together.

You make me hungry. So does writing this, if I'm honest. I am not sick when I look on you; I am starved. The relationship between a zombie and his food is quite complex. It is to be seen, to be sure. It must be seen. Looking on the eyes of the one you have loved as you feast is a sublime experience. There is no becoming together that compares to the satisfaction of feeding, feasting with a lover. Perhaps you've heard that eating brains induces the victim's memory to transfer into the one eating. That is partly right. However, it is also the savoring that breeds delight. Would that I could suffer in your stead, I imagine. But inevitably the thought just urges me forward: toward each tender morsel. Being together, having been together seems to season the flesh. Before and after.

How could I waste the best parts of my love? As fat as butter the best bits wait. How can I let one who I have loved so much go to the worms, or worse, to the horde? The one I have loved is to be preserved in me. As close to eternally as I can manage. Just when should one be eaten? Always is the answer. Best, the nearest. The most special feast comes from the one most dearly held. The darling lamb's softest parts the most appetizing. This is not to say, though, that others ought not get to participate. There is always good reason to expand one's palette.

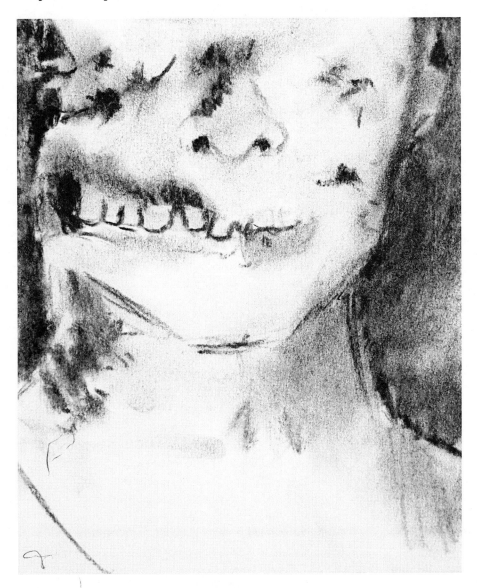

When the plague hit, the gnawing desire—always in the pit of the stomach—that had always drawn lovers near started working over-time. The need to consume each other simply transcended the metaphoric. Lovers know what it means to hunger for each other. They still do. It is equally clear that no loyalty can exist now save that held in mutual hunger. Taste is never to be foregone.

What was once relegated to the bedroom no longer requires hiding: taste reigns supreme in these days. Every moment is a choice, and it is always the same choice. Choosing ever which flesh to consume is precisely every day's exercise. It is the most satisfying—perhaps the only satisfying—event remaining. And why shouldn't it be? The exercise of taste is nothing new. God has given us will for precisely this reason. We must choose wisely. Each morsel screams its rightness as it makes its way inside. The constant press forward toward food blankets the silent moments of emptiness since the plague. Omnipresent comforter, it is all we must needs obey, all that must fill my mind. There is simple beauty in this, this one thing. Hunger.

You are the lord of my guts, the apple of my eye. I swear allegiance to every fiber of your flesh. I kneel before you. I serve you. Even as you serve me. We are eternally knit, allowing no impediment to hinder our love. More love. We banquet in the open streets—celebrating the joy that God has given us. At once together, and becoming. The still heart yet dripping with the glue that binds us, gracing our heart's table with the sweet flavor of red juices. Brain-fondness is perhaps our only proclivity remaining.

Never dead flesh, lumps of foul deformity. Never plague stricken goats. Only the living suffice. If your brain is as dry as a rice cake in a desert, it doesn't belong on my plate. I refuse. Besides, the chase is far more fun than it ever was. From our vantage, cloistered in the bush, we espy. Field dressing the prey no longer necessary, our feast is immediate! It is a holy communion cleaving us to each other and to every innocent who we share.

It seems so silly now that I was ever afraid to share this love with you. I feared, I admit. But having tasted the power and the pleasure, though I was an ungentle convert, I am a most fervent adherent. Looking back now on the earliest of these verses I hear the echoes of my former self. This life is rich. It is glazed in sauce fit for a queen. I would not trade for a moment the beauty that I now see everywhere. Angels! Earthly paragons! In every body the visage of the divine behind the eyes awaits.

In these my most confident moments I do not doubt that I bring glory to the world, though I deprive it of what may come. We live to taste the moment. And dear reader, I would be remiss if I did not leave you with a simple ode to that one most delicate and prized delicacy: brains. Never would I, never could I love with stomach, yet with the brain must I always engage. Its curls and curves slip most stealthily down. Take the heart, take the brain and weigh them; there are no equals. The sole arbiters of self and merit they weigh most heavily on the palate. It is the brain that nourishes the nerves. The brain that satisfies the soul. The brain matters. Whether my newest love's lamb-gentle brain or the still sparking brain of youth or the well-seasoned brain of time-tested philosophers, each globe satisfies infinitely. Unmix the brain with baser matter and it, alone, delights. Dine tonight, readers, and think on this. Hundreds of years hence these words remain potent to infect yet more brains, bridges toward infinity. For what cannot the brain coin that is for the goodness of humanity? Incomparable, inestimable, internalizable. Grief cannot survive outside the brain; grieve not for those who have succumbed, even as I am grateful. Rejoice, with me, in satisfaction.

XC

Then bite me when you will; if ever, now;
Now, while the world is bent double with loss,
Join with the spite of fortune, make me bow,
And do not drop in with a saving cross:
Ah! Don't, when my heart has escaped sorrow,
Come in the rearward like a conquered foe;
Give not windy night a rainy morrow,
To linger out a purposed overthrow.
If you will eat me, do not eat me last,
When other petty griefs have done their spite,
But in the onset feast: so shall I taste
At first the very worst of zombies' might;

27

And other strains of woe, which now seem woe,
Compared with loss of you, will not seem so.

LVIII

That God forbid, who made me first your slave,
I should in thought control your times of pleasure,
Or at your hand huge slabs of flesh to crave,
Being your vassal, bound to take your measure!
O! let me suffer, feeding on your back,
The imprisoned absence of your liberty;
And patience, from long suffering, taste each cheek,
Without accusing me of injury.
Be what you will, roast ribs rare, stew, or steak
That you yourself may privilege your taste
As you will; your tenderness never fake,
Pardon me, yourself, I cannot let waste.
I am to wait, though waiting so be hell,
I mustn't partake 'til you're medium well.

CX

Alas! It's true, I have fed here and there,
And made myself a mockery to view,
Gored my own friends, ripped through what is most dear,
Made old hurts into fresh bleeding wounds.
Most true it is, that I have looked on food
Askance and strangely; but, by all above,
These turnings showed my heart another good,
And worse delicacies proved my love.
Now all is done, save what shall have no end:
My appetite I never more will grind
On newer bones, rather than an old friend,
A god in love, to whom I am confined.
So give me welcome, next to heaven my best,
Even to your pure and most tasteful breast.

XXVI

Lord of my guts, to whom finest offal
Your merit has most deservedly fit
To you I send this written mouthful
To witness duty, not to show my wit:
Duty so great, which wit so poor this store
May make seem bare, in wanting words to show it,
But that I hope some good conceit of yours
In your soul's thought, all naked, will bestow it:
Till whatsoever star that guides my shambling,
Points on me graciously with fair aspect,
And puts apparel on my tattered loving,
To show me worthy of your sweet respect:
Then may I dare boast how I have eaten;
Till then, I'll hide my head: unworthy meat.

XXXVI

Let me confess that we two must seek brains,
Although our undivided skulls share one:
Or else those tastiest human remains,
Without my help, you will squander alone.
In our two minds there is but one aspect,
Though former lives a separable spite,
Now, since infection, seek just to infect
Yet then do we waste sweetmeats, our prizes right.
I must evermore acknowledge hunger,
Lest cannibalism should be my shame,
You must ever in this body linger,
Unless a cure takes z from out my name.
But I have come to love you in such sort
That we, being one, chase humans for sport.

XLVI

My eye and mouth are at a mortal war,
How to divide the conquest of your sight;

My eye my mouth your picture's bite would bar,
My mouth my eye the freedom of that right.
My mouth pleads his innards are worth a try,—
A closet never pierced with crystal eyes—
But the defendant that plea would deny,
And says in him your fair appearance lies.
Thus a jury needs to be impaneled
A quest for justice, all demand to start
And by their verdict is determined
The clear eye's portion, and the dear mouth's part:
As thus; my eye's due is your outward part,
My mouth's right to devour your loving heart.

L

How slowly do I shamble on the way,
When brains I seek, my weary travel's end,
Will teach that ease and that repose to say,
'Thus far the miles are measured from my food!'
The feet that bear me, tired with my woe,
Plod dully on, to bear that weight in me,
As if by instinct wretched me might know
This body loved not speed, being made zombie:
The bloody spur cannot provoke me on,
That sometimes anger thrusts into my hide,
Which heavily I answer with a groan,
More sharp to me than spurring to my side;
For that same groan has put this in my mind,
My food lies onward, and my life behind.

LXXXIV

Who is it that says most, which can say more,
Than this rich praise,—that you, alone, are you?
In whose confine immured is the store
Which should example where your equal grew.

Lean penury within that pen may dwell
That to his subject won't lend some small glory;
But he that writes of you, if he can tell
That you are you, so dignifies his story,
Let him but copy what in you is writ,
Not making worse what nature made so clear,
And such a counterpart shall fame his wit,
Making his style admired everywhere.
Yet with your beauteous blessings you curse,
Brains-fond, you punish poets with a hearse.

CIX

O! never say that I was false of heart,
Though gnawing seemed my flame to qualify,
As easy might I from myself depart
As from my soul which in your breast must lie:
That is my home of love: if I have ranged,
Like him who travels, returns to his house;
Until no single inch feels to him strange
Like that your self I come to nibble, spouse.
Never believe though in my nature reigned,
All frailties that besiege all kinds of blood,
That it could so preposterously be stained,
To leave for nothing all your sum of good;
For nothing in this universe I find,
Save you, my lamb, will hunger satisfy.

CXXXVII

You blind fool, Craving, how you deceive eyes,
That they behold, but don't see what they see?
They know what beauty is, see where it lies,
Yet what the worst is take the best to be.
If eyes, corrupt by foul zombic germs look,
Through opaque goggles thick scaled and unshied,

They see nothing that they don't seek to cook.
Or rather tear fresh off, oven untried.
Why should they espy not a single blot
Which all know to be the world's common place?
Yet mine eyes, hearing this, say this is not,
Beauty is found in each and every face.
So long as fresh brains behind, beating heart
Below: to this plague all beauty's tartare.

CXLII

Love is my sin, and your dear virtue hates,
All of my sin, grounded on sinful loving:
O! but with mine compare you your own state,
And you will find it scant merits reproving;
Or, if it do, not from your yet damp lips,
That have profaned their soft pink ornament
With, as oft as mine, scarlet flesh gobbets
Robbed from others' heads' revenues, their rents.
If it's lawful, I love you, as you love those
Whom your eyes pursue as mine to devour:
Root hunger in your heart, that, when it grows,
Your strong jaws may return what you deserve.
If you claim innocence and don't abstain,
By your example you your case profane.

CXLIV

Two loves I have of flesh fresh and meats sweet,
Which like two spirits animate me still:
The better taste is a brain's gray meat,
The worser flavor's flesh that's been long ill.
To win me soon to hell, my devil
Tempts my better angel from my side,
Corrupting me to be a cannibal,
Wooing my halves with succulent insides.

And though my angel be turned into fiend,
Suspect I may, yet not directly tell;
Each being both of me, I'm caught between,
Pursuing both, crafting another's hell.
Yet I can't prove without experiment
That fresh flesh and sweetmeats taste the same.

CLII

In chewing you like a kernel of corn
Surely I've heard memorable swearing
You appear twice: once at night, then the morn
Vowing new hate after new love bearing:
But why of two holes breach do I accuse you,
When I mouth twenty? I am perjured most;
For all my teeth are pearls for your sole misuse,
And all my honest faith in you is lost:
For I have made deep wounds of your deep kindness,
Riven your love, your truth, your constancy;
Even eaten your eyes to give you blindness,
Saving you from this plight that I must see.
For I swear you tender; more perjured I,
To swear against the truth so foul a lie!

3

Increase

These griefs and losses have so bated me
That I shall hardly spare a pound of flesh
To-morrow to my bloody creditor.
—Antonio, *The Merchant of Venice* (III.3)

So we've developed an oral fixation. It's true. But that's not to say that the desire to increase has ceased. The instrument of the symphony of love migrated up the body and now lives between the teeth. There is, you must admit, a certain beauty contained in the bite. Over, under, occasionally misaligned. Its individuality stands in for our own. The choice bite spreads the particular self. And so we feed. Contagiously. Continuously.

As ever, certain among us remain hungry for profit. Nothing, perhaps, will change that. Yet who could have conceived that a cottage industry of selling oneself up for biting would grow? That there could be status conferred by the one to do the biting? Sure enough, it matters who delivers the plague. And it matters as much who receives it. Discriminating amongst zombies? Yes. If one must turn, and indeed they must, why not select the deliverer? Youths and maidens sell themselves for the chance to be turned by someone great; they sell themselves to relieve their families of debt; they sell themselves because there are no other appetizing prospects for them to succeed in life beyond serving scullery. So of course status isn't the only reason to sell oneself. And debt is just as important. For the right first bite, families are willing to pay through the nose. The bite, the drive to increase, is the final, great, equalizer.

The ceremony surrounding the first bite has become every bit as

invested as a wedding. It is the new wedding, really. It commemorates the moment of turning from innocence to experience.

> I am a simple maid, and therein wealthiest
> That I protest I simply am a maid.
> Please it your Majesty, I have done already.
> The blushes in my cheeks thus whisper me:
> "We blush that thou shouldst choose; but, be refused,
> Let the white death sit on thy cheek for ever,
> We'll ne'er come there again."
> —Helena, *All's Well that Ends Well* [II.3]

Eighty nine mentions of blushing in my plays and poems. That's how many it took. That's how many I had. Oh, Helena! How I remember the dawning of knowledge on your cheeks. Never again, save the ever-savorings in my memory.

It didn't start out this way; then every single mention came to matter. The word memorializes each moment, each first bliss. Every one of those who I've had the fortune to bite blushes eternal: one blush for each of my progeny. Nothing can describe the beauty of the turning blush. Blood rushes to the cheeks, the first flush of fever. It is the first and among the last autonomic responses that ever show. It marks the reaping of the harvest. But this is about the harvest. About the increase. To be clear, we all know that we reap what we did not sow. And yet we must carry on for the good of all.

It is ever more important to preserve our kind now. Never before has there been such a predatory bunch seeking to destroy some part of the species. The foul living, brandishing their awful broadswords of destruction end our undeath so readily. We must respond—how could we not? Yet decidedly not all are amongst this group bent on destruction. The fair living far outnumber the foul.

Her second skin somehow accentuates rather than hides the full bloom of youth. Sensuous curves, each muscle ripples underneath the fleshy material. Palest peeks from the edges invite, no, beg further exploration. Flaxen angel's hair spins as she walks, faintly ruffled in the breeze. Grace itself lives in her fingers, gently playing over every object as she passes. Full lips and peeking teeth. Dance. Modesty comports subtle movements that, whether or not intended, seduce rather than suppress her inherent loveliness. Oh to taste the experience she holds within her! She is the very embodiment of desire; the perfect emblem of increase. She will carry far the burden of our race. Sooner perhaps than she might imagine.

The seeds of immortality in us war with the inevitability of mortality that has always plagued our species. Our species: we are still one. New, improved, remaining one. Nevertheless, entirely other. Selfless in a way that would have been impossible to conceive. And conceive we do.

The desire to spread is paramount. Even when it is no longer a matter of desire, the urgency drives us forward. Drive not desire. And yet, it is all consuming, this hunger. Does the weary traveler in the desert desire water? No more nor less than I desire to increase. And yet even so the beauty of our condition is its increase. Inspired toward infinity, hungry for the most tender morsels, we coalesce toward the same; moving bodies, warm, fluid, these are our hope and the delight of every day.

I do, too, remember my own first blush. What a glorious evening that was. It seems near an eternity ago, with the lines of a thousand characters written on my dropping body. Looking in the glass, I imagine my own ghastly appearance and give it voice through dear Warwick, who was but is no more:

> See how the blood is settled in his face.
> Oft have I seen a timely-parted ghost,
> Of ashy semblance, meagre, pale, and bloodless,
> Being all descended to the labouring heart,
> Who, in the conflict that it holds with death,
> Attracts the same for aidance 'gainst the enemy,
> Which with the heart there cools, and ne'er returneth
> To blush and beautify the cheek again.
> But see, his face is black and full of blood;
> His eye-balls further out than when he liv'd,
> Staring full ghastly like a strangled man;
> His hair uprear'd, his nostrils stretch'd with struggling;
> His hands abroad display'd, as one that grasp'd
> And tugg'd for life, and was by strength subdu'd.
> Look, on the sheets his hair, you see, is sticking;
> His well-proportion'd beard made rough and rugged,
> Like to the summer's corn by tempest lodged.
> —Warwick, *The Second Part of King Henry the Sixth* [III.2]

I am the tempest, I am the duke, I am the dead. Remembering back, I see her again. Herself driven to spread. And so I ask myself, what if my muse is a hungry muse?

C

> Where are you Muse that you forget so long,
> To taste of that which gives you all your might?
> Do you spend your fury on worthless song,
> Wasting your power to lend base subjects nights?

Return forgetful Muse, and straight redeem,
With massive numbers time so idly spent;
Chew the ears that won't give your teeth esteem
And fill your gut with skin and ligament.
Rise, hungry Muse! My love's sweet face survey,
If Time have any wrinkle graven there;
If any, be a satire to decay,
And make time's spoils despised neverwhere.
Give my love prey faster than Time wastes life,
Preventing the scythe and long needless strife.

CI

O truant Muse what will be your amend
For your neglect of truth in beauty dyed?
Both truth and beauty on my love depend;
So, too, are you quite therein dignified.
Make answer Muse: won't you happily say,
"Truth needs no color, with his color fixed;
Beauty no pencil, beauty's truth to lay;
But best is best, if never intermixed"?
Because he needs no praise, will you be dumb?
Excuse not neglect, for with you it lies
To make him much outlive a gilded tomb
And to be praised of ages yet to rise.
Then do your office, Muse; I'll teach you how
To make him walk long hence as he does now.

I

From fairest creatures we desire increase,
That thereby zombies' food might never die,
But as the riper should by time decease,
His tender heir might bear his memory:
But you contracted of the rife disease,
Feed your stomach with self-substantial fuel,
Making a famine where abundance lies,

38

Your kin your foe, to your sweet self too cruel:
You that are now the world's foul ornament,
And only herald to the rotting spring,
Within your own bud bury your content,
And tender chunks you make waste in hoarding:
Pity the world, or else be glutton true,
To eat the world's due, from the grave and you.

II

When forty walkers shall besiege your brow,
And dig deep trenches in your beauty's field,
Your youth's proud livery so grazed on now,
Will be a tattered taste of small worth held:
Then, being asked where all your beauty lies,
Where all the treasure of your lusty days;
To say, within your own deep sunken eyes,
Were an all-eating shame, and thriftless praise.
How much more praise deserved your beauty's taste,
If you could answer "This fair child of mine
Shall sum my count, and make hunger erased,"
Proving his value at targeting time!
This were to be new made when you do mold,
And see your blood stays in when it runs cold.

CXXXIII

Beshrew the nails that made my heart to groan
For that deep wound they gave my friend and me!
It's not enough to torture me alone,
But slave to slavery my sweetest friend must be?
Me from myself your cruel eye has taken,
And my next self you have harder engrossed:
Of him, myself, and you I am forsaken;
A torment thrice three-fold thus to be crossed:
You vacated my soul with your hands scarred,
Then ate my friend's big heart before the turn;

Whoever sees me, let my moans be his guard;
He will not then find rigor in return.
Yet you, reader, will; I, hungry for you,
Perforce am yours, and you are all my due.

CXXXIV

So, now I must confess that he is gone,
And I myself am mortgaged to disease,
Myself I'll forfeit, so that other mine
You will restore my comfort my release:
But you will not, nor can cure set him free,
He tried friend-like to give his life for mine
Under the bond that bound him fast as me
Yet you are covetous, and he is blind.
The statute of his beauty fast taken
You usurer, you put forth all to use,
Who plagued my friend came debtor for my sake;
So him I lost through willing sacrifice.
Him have I lost; you have both him and me:
He pays the whole, and yet I am not free.

CXXXV

Will flies with vacant self, yet you have "Will,"
And "Will" to boot, and "Will" in over-plus;
More than enough am I that vexed you still,
To your sweet will making addition thus.
Will you, whose will is large and spacious,
Not once vouchsafe to hide my will in yours?
Shall will in others seem right gracious,
And in my will no fair acceptance source?
The sea, all water, yet receives rain still,
And in abundance still adds to his store;
So you, being rich in "Will," add to your "Will"
One will of mine, to make your large will more.
Now, since you must, it's time to face the kill:
Though you've more choices, the best choice is "Will."

CV

Let not my love be called idolatry,
Nor my beloved as an idol show,
Since all alike my songs and praises be
To one, of one, still such, and ever so.
Kind is my love today, tomorrow kind,
Still constant in a wondrous excellence;
Therefore my verse to constancy confined,
One thing expressing, leaves out difference.
'Love, feed, and spread,' is all my argument,
'Love, feed, and spread,' varying to other words;
And in this change is my invention spent,
Three themes in one, which wondrous scope affords.
'Love, feed, and spread,' have often lived alone,
Which three till now, never kept seat in one.

LXXXVI

Was it the proud full sail of his great verse,
Bound for the prize of all too precious you,
That did my ripe thoughts in my brain inhearse,
Making their tomb the womb wherein they grew?
Was it his spirit, by spirits taught to write,
Above a mortal pitch, that struck me dead?
No, neither he, nor his compeers by night
Giving him aid, my verse astonished.
He, nor that affable familiar ghost
Which nightly gulls him with intelligence,
As victors of my silence cannot boast;
I was not sick of any fear from thence:
But when your countenance succumbed to dine,
Unnaturally, then that enfeebled mine.

CXVII

Accuse me thus: that I have bitten all,
Wherein I should your great desserts repay,

Forgot upon your dearest love to call,
Whereto all bonds do tie me day by day;
That I have frequent bitten unknown minds,
And given to time your own dear-purchased right;
That I have hoisted sail to all the winds
Which should transport me farthest from your sight.
Write both my willfulness and errors down,
And on just proof surmise, accumulate;
Bring me within the level of your frown,
But shoot not at me in your wakened hate;
I plead guilty to forgetting my vow
Yet fear not: I return my duty now!

XVI

But wherefore do not you, a mightier way,
Make war upon this bloody tyrant, Time?
And fortify your self in your decay
With means more fatted than my barren rhyme?
Now feast at the bar during happy hours,
And many maiden gardens, yet unset,
With carnivorous wish taste living flowers,
To reproduce your painted counterfeit:
So should the lines of life that life repair,
Which this, cannibal jaws, your hunger then,
Neither inward restrained nor outward fair,
Can make you gorge your self on eyes of men.
To feast upon one's love, keeps yourself fill,
And you must live, fed by your own sweet Will.

LXIV

When I have seen by Time's fell hand defaced
The rich-proud cost of outworn buried age;
When grounds open to reveal the down-razed,
New made eternal slaves to mortal rage;
When I have seen the hungry ocean gain

Advantage on the kingdom of the shore,
And unfirm flesh drip with its gory stain
Increasing store with loss, and loss with store;
When I have seen such interchange of state,
Or state itself confounded, to decay;
Ruin hath taught me thus to ruminate—
That Time will come and take my love away.
Or worse, it will not. Death we cannot choose
So we live, before time and life we lose.

XCVII

A nuclear winter my absence has been
From you, the pleasure of the fleeting year!
What freezings have I felt, what dark days seen!
What old December's bareness everywhere!
And yet this time removed was summer's prime;
Teeming autumn, swelling with rich increase,
Bearing my gross burden of new-dead time,
Infesting worms dining on ripe decease:
Yet this abundant feast seemed to me born
Of wasted hope and still unpicked green fruit;
For summer and his pleasures wait forlorn,
Since you're alive, keeping vultures quiet.
  Or, if they call, it's with so dull a cheer,
  That leaves us pale, dreading the winter's near.

CIV

To me, fair friend, you never can be old,
For as you were when first your eye I eyed,
Such seems your beauty still. Three winters cold
Your form endured shaking flesh from your side;
Your beauteous spring to yellow fall's turned,
In process of the seasons have I seen,
Three April perfumes in three hot Junes burned,
Since first I saw you fresh, which yet are green.

43

Ah! yet does beauty like a clock-hand,
Steal from his figure, and no pace perceived;
So your sweet hue, which I think still must stand,
Has motion, and my eye may be deceived:
For fear of which, hear this you age unbred:
Ere you were born was beauty's summer dead.

CXXVI

O you, my Barbra, who in your power
Tight holds Time's fickle glass, his fickle hour;
Who has by waning grown, and therein shows
Your lover's withering, as your sweet self grows.
If Nature, sovereign mistress over wrack,
As you go onwards, still will pluck you back,
She keeps you for this purpose, that her skill
May time disgrace and wretched minutes kill.
Yet fear her, O you minion of her pleasure!
She may detain, but not still keep, her treasure:
Her audit (though delayed) answered must be,
Her quietus is to render you Z.

XXII

Mirrors shall not persuade me I am old,
So long as youth and you are of one date;
But when on your face rot's furrows I behold,
Then I'll beg death my days' end to haste.
For the beauty that covers your body,
Is the simple fine clothing of my heart
Living in your chest as yours lives in me
How can I then be older than you are?
O! therefore, love, be of yourself so wary
As I, not for myself, but for you try;
Having swallowed your heart, cooked so rarely
And as tender any wagyu ribeye.
Don't seek your heart when cure remakes us men
I've eaten yours not to give back again.

4

Life's Better as a Zombie

Poor worm, thou art infected!
This visitation shows it.
—Prospero, *The Tempest* (III.1)

From somewhere to somewhere else. If nothing else, this story is one of transition. Everyone begins somewhere; each of my zombie loves began with me in the world that is no more. When the plague began, fear gripped humankind. As time passed and the world went on in its post-apocalyptic stage, the ranks of the plague-ridden grew as numerous as the stars in heaven. The transformation of the world began to be seen as a boon rather than a disaster. But to me, to mine, it was always clear.

There is no question that this state is worthy of praise, more organized than the hive, more fair than any democracy. I want to sing the praise of egalitarianism: we live as equals now, in both theory and practice. The transfiguration of power has put an end to discord and suffering. The Queen is still the head of the country—even the world. We are still the body. Yet the power that she wields is not the same as it was. There is no need to persecute those conspiring toward sedition. There is no more sedition.

We all share authority now. Authority comes from the very substance of our blood. The order of succession passes through the tooth. The time for anxiety over authority has gone and all can rest assured of their future, political and otherwise. The law itself is suspended and we operate according to a new order, functioning entirely outside the written law. Because we share authority, there is no more unnecessary violence. There is no jockeying for power and no back biting.

None are stabbed in the back or poisoned while they sleep with a leprous distilment of hebona in the ear. None must await behind a curtain to oversee the vestiges of madness. None seek revenge.

There is furthermore an end to the lease of control on life. Whatever the length of the lease, the time has expired. The threat of the

inevitable has become, instead, the order of the moment. What does it mean to have a lease of control on life? It means that we must succumb. There may be an option to extend control, perhaps even beyond the span of a lifetime. Yet there is never so much that we might actually take possession of the control of a life, ours or other. We are responsible only to a point, and that point is fixed before and after our time. The fantasy of control becomes ever so obvious from the other side: when one is driven onward, craving. It is in this honesty that life—or whatever this is that has replaced it—became worthwhile.

To be known. That is all. And it has become intimately, ultimately, inevitably possible. When the veil that made it impossible rent, then. That there is no past tense of rend is lamentable. The rending of the veil is the most precious end of the apocalypse. The rending of its bodies is the substance of the life. The plague is one of purification—it makes of flesh the curtain in favor of that which will not become food for the worm.

Knowledge has become status. Salvation salivation. Consuming the knowledge of the other has become a chance to get to know the other, from within her or his boots. The knowing of others is the sole source of status now, it is the means of distinction in the horde no matter how far flung we may be. The intimacy of experience and its infinity is the substance of the furtherance of existence. This is the reason to go on. The drug of choice. The reason that we share to move forward day by day, sunset through sunrise.

Potency is the kind of power that results in the loss of blood; it is the substance behind decapitation and drawing and quartering. Those are the punishments for Catholicism these days. Bloody Mary was a horror. Her successor mighty and far more terrible. When my mother's cousin, William Arden, lost his head: it fell at the feet of potent power, too terrible to allow freedom to dissent. All those brains gone to waste; the shame bellows from the grave. And that is not even the worst of it. Don't imagine for a minute, reader, that the apocalypse is even a hair's breadth worse than what came before, at least in terms of bloodshed. You've heard of Bloody Mary, I trust? Do you know of drawing and quartering, reader?

Marian reforms set the stage for our Glorious Queen, *Fidei Defensor*. She was indeed the defender of the faith and she remains so, though perhaps the nature of the faith itself has altered fundamentally. The object of faith is now so much more immediate and tangible. To the tooth, one might say. Long live the *Zombie Defensor*. Long live the horde. As much as Elizabeth has retained her self she deserves the title. She has brought as many into the fold as a good shepherd at dusk.

But from these musings I must turn closer to home, toward my own flock. With the tiniest fingers and still unseeing eyes he reached up and clung to me. Each startle, arms flung outward, impossibly strong grip tightening, makes me smile ever yet. In this hungry world the only place for him to survive is in these words, in memory mingled with desire, the dead earth's bloom growing up from dull roots in spring rain.

> O all you host of heaven! O earth! What else?
> And shall I couple hell? Hold, hold, my heart!
> And you, my sinews, grow not instant old,
> But bear me stiffly up. Remember thee?
> Ay, thou poor ghost, while memory holds a seat
> In this distracted globe.
> —Hamlet, *Hamlet* [I.5]

This wasteland is ideally suited for the gruesome and the memory of tiny fingers and toes stays safe locked within this vault. The syrup poured over the earth will never dye your skin; you will never meet the throngs of the faithful arrayed for the spectacle. The world can be, is, at peace.

The distance between what we were and what we are feels insurmountable. This world is impossible. It is the impossible come to being in the everyday. If my plays have tread on anything it is that no human has her or his life together. If comedy rings untrue it is precisely for this reason: it is not only fantastical, it is temporary. There can be no ever after outside of the momentary interruption of the stage. Or, there couldn't have been. Now we face ever after. Now peace is lasting. Zombie ever after.

XI

As fast as you shall rot, so fast you grow,
In one of yours, from that which you've had to go;

And fresh offal which youngly you had taste,
You may call yours when you from life convert,
Herein lives wisdom, beauty, and increase;
Without this folly, age, and cold decay:
If all were minded so, the times should cease
And all would willingly join World War Z.
Let those whom nature hath not made for store,
Harsh, featureless, and rude, barrenly perish:
Look, whom she best endowed, she gave you more;
Which bounteous gift you should in bounty cherish:
She scratched you for her meal, and meant thereby,
You should taste more, not let that dinner die.

LXX

Your blame does not from your beauty detract
Though viral scars can worst deface the fair;
The ornament of beauty is suspect,
A crow that flies in heaven's sweetest air.
And when one's too high, slander clearly floods
Drowning the very best one at a time;
For disease preys upon the sweetest buds,
And you presented a pure unstained prime.
You have passed by the ambush of young days
Either not poisoned, or victor being charged;
Yet this your praise cannot be so your praise,
To tie up envy, evermore enlarged,
If some contagious ill ignored your face,
Then for you alone every heart would waste.

XXIX

When in disgrace, past fortune and men's eyes
I all alone weep for my withered state,
And trouble deaf heaven with my worthless cries,
And look upon myself, and curse my fate,

Wishing me like to one more rich in hope,
Featured like him, like him with friends possessed,
Desiring this man's will, and that man's scope,
With what I most enjoy contented least;
Yet in these thoughts myself almost despising,
Haply I think of you,— and then my state,
Like to the corpse at break of night arising
From sullen earth, singing hymns at heaven's gate;
For your sweet love remembered such wealth brings
That then I'd scorn to trade my death for living.

XXXVIII

How can my muse want subject to invent,
While undead roam, pouring into my verse
Their own foul argument, too abhorrent
For all but the cavity of a hearse?
O! give yourself the thanks, if something here
Worth perusing finds itself in your sight
For who is so dumb that cannot write cheer,
But in this—you yourself invent the fright.
Perhaps you're the tenth Muse, ten times more worth
Than those old nine which rhymers invocate;
And he that calls on you, let him bring forth
Eternal numbers to outlive long date.
If my slight muse please these curious days,
The pain is mine, but yours shall be the praise.

LII

So am I as the rich, whose blessed key,
Can bring him to his sweet locked-up treasure,
The which he will not every hour survey,
For blunting the fine point of seldom pleasure.
Therefore are feasts so solemn and so spaced,
Since, seldom coming, apart they must set,

Like gems of worth they're so sparingly placed,
Victims are now so thin and infrequent.
So is the time that keeps you for my chest,
Or the wardrobe which hides the robe within,
To make some special instant special-blest,
That moment when you join me for dinner.
Then blessed are those who hunger and thirst,
For we will be filled, with your giblets first.

XCII

But do your worst to steal yourself away,
For the term of life you are assured mine;
And life no longer than your love will stay,
For mine depends upon your love, its sign.
Then I need not fear becoming undead:
Rather than meet a sad and lonely end
I see a better state to me than dread
Since life doesn't on you or their teeth depend:
You cannot vex me with inconstant mind,
They cannot tear my heart to death with lies
O! what a happy title do I find,
Happy to have your love, happy to die!
But what's so blessed-fair that fears no blot?
You may be false, and yet I know it not.

XCIII

So shall I live, supposing you are you,
Like a deceived husband; so love's face
May still seem love to me, though altered new;
Your looks with me, your brain in other place:
For there can live no hatred in your eye,
Therefore in that I cannot know your change.
In many's looks, the false heart's history
Is writ in wounds, and frowns, and scratches strange.

51

But heaven in your creation did decree
That in your face sweet love should ever dwell;
Whatever your thoughts, or your heart's workings be,
Your looks should nothing else save sweetness tell.
How like Eve's apple does your beauty shift,
Despite the change toward hue of granny smith.

XCIV

They that have power to hurt, and will do none,
That do not do the thing they threaten most,
Who, moving others, are themselves as stone,
Rigid, cold, never to temptation lost;
They rightly do inherit heaven's graces,
And hold to nature's riches despite all;
They are the lords and owners of their faces,
Others but stewards heralding human fall.
The summer's flower is to the summer sweet,
Though to itself, it only live and die,
But if that flower with base infection meet,
The basest weed outbraves his dignity:
For sweetest things turn sourest by their deeds;
Lilies that fester smell far worse than weeds.

CIII

Alack! what poverty my Muse brings forth,
That having such a scope to show her pride,
The argument, all bare, is of more worth
Than when it has my added praise beside!
O! blame me not, if I no more can write!
Look in your mirror: there appears a face
That exceeds my blunt invention quite,
Dulling my lines, and doing me disgrace.
Were it not sinful then, striving to mend,
To mar the subject risen straight from hell?
For to no other Z my verses tend

Than your grave graces and your gifts to tell;
And more, much more, than in my verse can sit,
Your own glass shows you when you look in it.

CXV

Those lines that I wrote before are all lies.
Even those that said I could not love you dearer:
Yet then my judgment knew no reason why
My most full flame should afterwards burn clearer.
But reckoning taste, whose million flavors
Creep up chimneys, and change decrees of kings,
Roast sacred beasts, tempt even the Savior,
Divert strong minds toward experimentings;
Alas! why fearing of taste's tyranny,
Might I not then say, "Now I love you best,"
When I was certain on uncertainty,
Crowning the present, doubting of the rest?
Love is a bite, then might I not give rhyme,
Better cooked and eaten than ravaged by time.

CXLV

Those lips that Love's own hand did make,
Breathed forth the sound that said "I hate"
To me that languished for her sake:
But when she saw my woeful state,
Straight in her heart did mercy come,
Chiding that tongue that ever sweet
Was used in giving gentle doom;
And taught it thus anew to greet;
'I hate' she altered with an end,
That followed it as gentle day,
Doth follow night, who like a fiend
From heaven to hell is flown away.
"I hate…" from hate away she freed,
And saved my life, saying "…zombies."

5

Time

'Tis now the very witching time of night,
When churchyards yawn, and hell itself breathes out
Contagion to this world. Now could I drink hot blood
And do such bitter business as the day
Would quake to look on.
—Hamlet, *Hamlet* (III.2)

At the end of time, we will all be the same: lusterless vile jelly. Until, years and years hence, unpreserved, we will blow into the wind and dust the earth or green its gardens. In the meantime, yawning churchyards yield their tender wards. The rising and the setting of the sun have ceased to mean as they did.

When days and nights first began to blend, you had just turned. Only the day before every bit of your self had been for me. There was in every second the sense of reward undeserved and the thrill of a chance encounter grown into love. You stood on the craggy mountain between heaven and earth—outside the city, wearing clouds as your ringlets, your radiance lighting the horizon. Dawn or dusk it didn't matter for you were the sun. The image lives on in my mind, calling up the time when we were together, now again highlighting that you are gone, that the moment is no more. Time has become shorthand for this moment. Now and again I would turn it back to undo what has been lost, to remake you and me. Time will not return at my beckoning.

Time is the inescapable illusion, pressing itself onto our days. Minute by minute, waves never-ending lap onto the shores of our existence, completely invisible as they happen. The weight of time is not its momentary passing but its accumulation into years and life-times. Birthdays in and of themselves don't measure the passing of time, but it is the sum of all birthdays that make a life shape incontro-vertibly the substance of our lives. Of my life. Now I am immortal, or at least I pretend to be. The immediate sting of death is off, the bee already shed its threat. It is now only the sum of the lapping of time that threatens as the infinity of slow rotting still inevitably draws every speck of matter toward the ground. I am pulled like a bent thorn overhung with moss, never speedily—grain by grain—toward

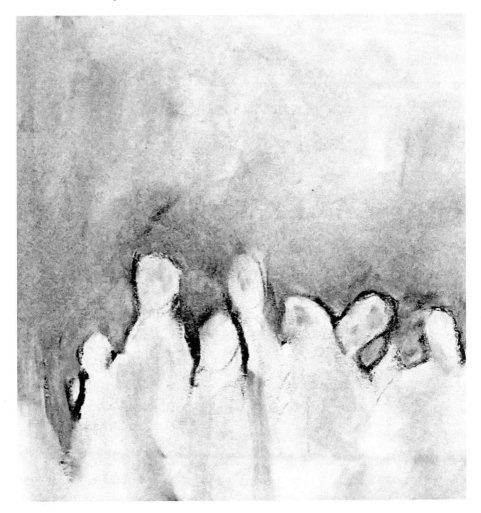

the grave. Thus is apocalyptic time. This is apocalyptic time. There is the infinite possibility of hope even alongside, ever alongside, the infinite certainty of dissolution. It is a contradiction in terms.

Ahh, then there is another fissure in the hourglass. The passage of time, ever less straightforward than seems apparent, has now entirely abdicated its arc. Clearly it still presses onward and yet it has become infinitely tangential. Moments spark, brief flashes of lightning extend from the dial, crisscrossing monotony. Dinner by dinner, flesh by flesh, the calendar advances into the future.

Even so the creases that rive the corners of mouths need never again drive us toward strange practices of denial. Hands grown spotted with sun and liver failure are very nearly as tasty as those fresh and unsullied. Spring chicken and textured old bird are perfect complements for the insatiate.

> Do I contradict myself?
> Very well then I contradict myself,
> (I am large, I contain multitudes.)
> —Walt Whitman, "Song of Myself"

Yes. I am not the first nor the last; I am fearless and I am nevertheless undone. I am ever of two minds. I have made multitudes one with myself and one with our cause. My teeth and every atom of my blood testify to the strength of the multitude. I remain in the world though I no longer live in it. I remember the world and I memorialize its wonder even as I fade from it. Every moment that passes is part of infinity and the substance itself of forever.

Zombie stories have always been about facing our own mortality, throwing back the mortal veil in order to live. The zombie visage is a glass; mirrored in it we see the manifest image of some obscure part of our own imagination. Even framed in glass, the image betrays its fragility. Even as we envision the submerged self, we threaten to destroy it with excess trauma, defacing violence that threatens to unhinge all that we have come to know as social order.

Then we are betrayed as abject souls thrown together into the graduated cauldron of time. Stewed together. Our individual flavors, as if through osmosis, passing from one to the other.

Words alone perhaps threaten to overtake the glass of time. In the infinite beginning, formless and void, words reverberated through the epoch of darkness. Age by age they persist, wriggling and thriving and slippery—altering bland passage with a map of continuity.

Palsied hands hold the promise of every human's end. Even those lucky enough to survive the diseases of childhood and the ravages of adulthood have only the promise of slowly-dissolving self-control. There is in every life lived the stuff of memory and that which is worth saving for posterity, but make no mistake: every end comes with a corpse confrontation. So what? Every family has figured out a way to care for Great Aunt Jule, long since unable to even chew her own food. She still anchors the family tent on festival days, connecting the great grandchildren to their own pasts. The tinge of sadness and horror that always comes with a chance meeting, when she plucks their cheeks, when she kisses them on the forehead—the smell of death in life that betrays her as past her prime need no longer frighten the young.

There is in these verses a space for time to be bleak and those still caught in its passage to be hopeful. There is hope for those who have already exited its clutches, its insidious claws no longer threaten.

Those who came before, the countless burden of the earth for whom time has already ceased, weigh on the living in moments of shattered peace. There is no rest promised or implied. There is only ever the present, accompanied by these verses that will stand the test of time—even beyond living rot.

LX

Like as the waves make towards the pebbled shore,
So do our minutes hasten to their end;
Each changing place with that which goes before,
In sequence driving with death to contend.
Nativity, once the lit hope of night
Crawls to maturity, until, being crowned,
Evil forces against his glory fight,
And Time that gave seeks only to confound.
Time transfixes the flourish set on youth
And delves the corn rows into beauty's brow,

Zak feeds on nature's delicacies smooth,
And nothing stands but for his maw to mow:
And yet in times without hope, my verse stands.
Praising life's worth, despite his cruel hand.

LIX

If there be nothing new, and that which is
Hath been before, how are our brains beguiled,
Which, laboring for invention, seek amiss
The harrowing burden of hunger wild?
O! that record could with a backward look,
Even of five thousand years of our race,
Show me Z's image in some antique book,
Since mind at first in humankind was placed!
That I might see what the old world could say
To this composed wonder of our shame;
Where we are worse, or how fared better they,
Or whether revolution be the same.
Sure I ingest wits of those former days,
But their same savagery here wins malaise.

V

Short hours, that with tender moments youth frame
On which the gaze of hungry eyes long dwell,
Will play the tyrants to the very same
And that unfair which fairly still excels;
For never-resting time leads summer on
To hideous winter, and confounds him there;
Sap checked with frost, and lusty leaves quite gone,
Beauty o'er-snowed and bareness everywhere:
Then were not summer's distillation left,
A liquid prisoner pent in Tupperware,
Beauty's effect with beauty were bereft,
Nor it, nor no remembrance of its fair:

But brains stewed, though they with winter meet,
Lease but their show; their substance still lives sweet.

XII

When I do count the clock that tells the time,
And see the brave day sunk in hideous night;
When I behold the violet past prime,
And sable curls, all moldering with blight;
When lofty trees I see barren of leaves,
Which erst from heat did canopy the herd,
And summer's green all girded up in sheaves,
Borne on the bier with white and bristly beard,
Then of you, beauty, do I question make,
That you among the wastes of time must go,
Since sweets and beauties do themselves forsake
And die as fast as they see others grow;
Nothing against Time's scythe can make defense
Save breed: to repopulate when you're hence.

LVI

Sweet love, renew your force; be it not said
Your edge should be blunter than appetite,
Which but daily by feeding is allayed,
Tomorrow sharpened in his former might:
So, love, be you, although today you fill
Your hungry eyes, even till they wink with fullness,
Tomorrow see again, and do not kill
The spirit of love, with a perpetual dullness.
Let this sad interim like the ocean be
Which parts the shore, where two contracted new
Come daily to the banks, that when they see
Return of love, more blest may be the view;
We've survived together apocalypse,
Let not hunger or boredom turn these lips.

LXVI

Tired with all these, for restful death I cry,
For such times as this were no humans born,
The needy with nothing trimmed in tears dry,
And purest faith unhappily forsworn,
And gilded honor shamefully misplaced,
And maiden virtue rudely strumpeted,
And right perfection wrongfully disgraced,
And strength by limping sway disabled
And art made tongue-tied by authority,
And folly—doctor-like—controlled with skill,
And simple truth miscalled simplicity,
And captive good attending captain ill:
Tired with all these, to Zs would I succumb,
Save that, on death, for my love I'd be chum.

CXIII

Since I passed on, my eye is in my mind;
And that which governs me to go about
Does part his function and is partly blind,
Seems seeing, but effectually is out;
For it no form delivers to the heart
Of bird, of flower, or meal that it just snatched:
Of his quick objects hath the mind no part
Nor his own vision holds what it can catch;
For if it see the rudest or gentlest sight,
The most sweet favor or deformed creature,
The mountain or the sea, the day or night:
The crow, or dove, it shapes them to your feature.
Incapable of more, consumed with brains,
My most true mind thus mine untrue feigns.

CXIV

Perhaps my mind, being crowned with thoughts of you,
Drinks up the monarch's plague, this flattery?

Or maybe shall I say, my eye says true,
And that your love taught it this alchemy,
To make of monsters and things indecent
Such angels as your sweet self resembles,
Creating every bad a perfect best,
As fast as objects to his beams assemble?
O! It's the first, it's flattery in my seeing,
And my great mind most kingly drinks it fresh:
My eye well knows what with his taste agrees
And to his palate well prepares the flesh:
If it be your body, it's hardly sin
That my eye loves it and does first bite in.

6

Apocalyptic Living

Be absolute for death; either death or life
Shall thereby be the sweeter. Reason thus with life.
If I do lose thee, I do lose a thing
That none but fools would keep. A breath thou art,
Servile to all the skyey influences,
That dost this habitation where thou keep'st
Hourly afflict. Merely, thou art Death's fool;
For him thou labour'st by thy flight to shun
And yet run'st toward him still. Thou art not noble;
For all th' accommodations that thou bear'st
Are nurs'd by baseness. Thou'rt by no means valiant;
For thou dost fear the soft and tender fork
Of a poor worm. Thy best of rest is sleep,
And that thou oft provok'st; yet grossly fear'st
Thy death, which is no more. Thou art not thyself;
For thou exists on many a thousand grains
That issue out of dust. Happy thou art not;
For what thou hast not, still thou striv'st to get,
And what thou hast, forget'st. Thou art not certain;
For thy complexion shifts to strange effects,
After the moon. If thou art rich, thou'rt poor;
For, like an ass whose back with ingots bows,
Thou bear'st thy heavy riches but a journey,
And Death unloads thee. Friend hast thou none;
For thine own bowels which do call thee sire,
The mere effusion of thy proper loins,
Do curse the gout, serpigo, and the rheum,
For ending thee no sooner. Thou hast nor youth nor age,
But, as it were, an after-dinner's sleep,
Dreaming on both.... What's yet in this
That bears the name of life? Yet in this life
Lie hid moe thousand deaths; yet death we fear,
That makes these odds all even.
—The Duke, *Measure for Measure* (III.1)

Though we live unfit for any place but hell, we make for ourselves a heaven of this hell. We hasten toward the end of this season rushing hourly toward the end of affliction. Until we aren't; when we've learned to make accommodation to death, when we've learned to be his bedfellow there is no longer a need to rush. There is room to savor, to breathe deep the breath of life. We can now savor even harsh moments. Hunger makes meals sweeter; thirst, wine richer. Undeath makes life—real life—that much more precious. Every moment becomes precious. Whilst before there was a constant press toward the end of time, there is now luxury in felt moments. Now we are no death's fools. Now, no longer threatened by the fork of the worm, we are free to focus on our own feeding. The burden has lifted and the journey has become the reason for existence. Hour by hour we grow more, not less, rich. Disease has squandered the time of its threat. It is as impotent as a hundred-years dotard. No thousand deaths lurk; we die to live!

Even so, ever so, I long for the absolute of death. I fear it even yet. There is no possibility of absolute. This is no longer a world of absolutes, if it ever were. What are we—who am I—but a physical manifestation of uncertainty in the world. We are the very tangible product of a world unable to come to terms with itself, with its own ends. Or, rather, not a world but a species. We fear the reality of death, a condition that we are completely unable to process. We ceremonialize it. We spectacularize it. Its experience is impossible. And yet it constantly haunts us. In our deepest fears, our darkest dreams, we cannot engage. It is always just out of reach, like the tastiest morsel, that we must nevertheless seek desperately to grasp every moment.

Every wall seems black, the soot of a thousand chimneys coloring the faces of the buildings to match the faces spewing forth from them. The char houses stink, now almost exclusively full of the victims too much devoured to turn. Would that I could describe it for you such that your nostril could make of it a scratch and sniff.

What does it mean to live together in an apocalyptic time? There are three markers that mark these apocalyptic days.

Constant compulsion is the first. Creeping constantly, ever toward my next meal, the infinite variety of thoughts that would have

accompanied my everyday has diminished. Variety has not vanished, it is just now tinged with Epicurean fantasy. This is the life emptied of all pain; it is a vision of pure happiness. Nevertheless, all hinges on the presence of mental disturbance. There is and there is not cause for mental disturbance. Regularly expected and achieved satisfaction is my state. It is happiness incarnate even with the constant press toward the next bite.

Sleeplessness is the second. Never is there a moment of rest.

Every day night hath been too brief. The venom coursing through my veins poisons the day and night's darkness obscures the substance of my dreams. Perhaps it is true that both the dead and the living sleep. The dead sleep in eternal rest. The living sleep the span of a night and awaken refreshed. The undead sleep in dis-ease.

Longing is the third. Omnipresent longing to see you. To press flesh on flesh. That there might be an other with whom I can be is the longing of the apocalypse. The longing of living in undeath. Every cracked smile hints at the possibility that persists just out of reach. Make no mistake: no irrational desire haunts the undead. I long for simple pleasures: the lust of the body in all its forms. There is naught to weigh beyond the ache in my body. The amputated totality of my soul gives way to the press of my gut. Yet, still, I love and I remember, from somewhere deeply woven into the fabric of my soul. Fixity upon fixity persist to shape remembrance of some infinite good that remains as the substance of unperished longing below conscious desire.

Lingering on, a vestige of a world gone by, I physically persist. I mentally persist, the vestige of the world gone by lingers in me. I live for the present, always hungry—longing for flesh—for the heart of my Juliet—always insatiate. I am woven of the weakness of a changing body, unenduring flesh tethered to a fixity that is not now nor ever was. The world is fixed. Persistence of past and future made present extends the possibility of forever. This marks the day to day of apocalyptic living. This is the daily practice. Of increase I must write.

The threat of jaws for the living is constant. There can be no relief.

XXVII

Weary with life, I hasten toward death
The dear repose for limbs with travel tired;
But then begins the never ending quest
To work my shape, when my mind's work's expired:
For then my thoughts—from far where I abide—
Intend a zealous pilgrimage to be,

Yours! Keep my drooping eyelids open wide,
Looking on darkness which the blind do see:
Save that my soul's imaginary sight
Presents your shadow to my sightless view,
Which, like a brain hung in ghastly night,
Makes black night beauteous, and her old face new.
Lo! thus, by day my limbs, by night my teeth,
Vestigial, toward you creep to wrest peace.

XXVIII

How can I then survive the daily fight,
When I am barred from benefit of rest?
When day's oppression is not eased by night,
But day by night and night by day oppressed,
And each, though enemies to either's reign,
In consent shake hands to be my torture,
The one by toil, the other to complain
How far I toil, still farther off from you.
I tell the day, to please him you are bright,
With green irradiated skin glowing
So I flatter the swart-complexioned night,
When sparkling stars dim, you gild the evening.
But day daily draws my sorrows stronger,
And night nightly makes grief's length seem longer.

XLIII

When most I squint, then my drooped eyes see true,
For all the day they view vile things infected;
But when I sleep, in dreams they look on you,
And darkly bright, are bright in dark directed.
Then you, whose shadow shadows most make bright,
How much your shadow's form forms happy show
To the clear day with your much clearer light,
When to unseeing eyes your shade shines so!

Long gone from eyes my eyes protest betrayed
By looking on you in the living day,
When in dead night your fair imperfect shade
Through heavy sleep on sightless eyes will stay!
All days are nights to see till you I see,
And nights bright days when dreams show you to me.

XLIV

If the dull gobbets of my flesh were sought,
Injurious distance could not stop your way;
For then despite the space I would be brought,
From limits far remote, wherever you stray.
No matter then although my foot will stand
Upon the farthest earth removed from here;
For nimble hordes can wade both sea and land,
As soon as think the place they would be there.
But, ah! thought kills me that I am not thought,
To leap large lengths of miles when you are gone,
But that so much of earth and water wrought,
I must attend my hovel with my moan;
Receiving naught for parts' decay to slow
But heavy tears, badges of foregone woe.

LXXXV

My tongue-out Muse whose sagging jaws can't hide
The evidence of your temperament riled
Gnashing pearls and golden fillings beside
Whose precious lips now droop apart unsmiled.
I think good thoughts, while others write good words,
And like unlettered fools still cry "Amen"
To every hymn that able spirit affords,
In polished form of well-refined pen.
Recalling your praise, I say "it's still true,"
And to the most of praise add something more;

But that is in my thought, whose love to you,
Though the world's end's come, holds forevermore.
Then others, whose eyes might come to see true
Cannot make my words deny love for you.

LXXXIX

Say that you forsake me for some dire fault,
And I will agree upon that offence:
Speak of my lameness, and I straight will halt,
Against your reasons making no defense.
You cannot, love, disgrace me half so ill,
Wishing my mind toward its final derange,
As I'll myself disgrace; knowing your will,
I'll acquaintance savor, and you estrange;
Be absent from your haunts; and on my tongue
Your sweet beloved taste no more lingers,
Lest I, too much profane, should do you wrong,
Having our acquaintances for dinner.
For you, against myself I'll vow debate,
For I must never love him whom you hate.

XCI

Some glory in fortresses, some in skill,
Some in their wealth, some in their body's force,
Some in their kevlar, though new-fangled ill;
Some in their hounds and bling, some in their hearse;
And every taste corresponds to pleasure,
Wherein it finds a joy above the rest:
But these particulars are not my measure,
All these I better in one general best.
Your love is better than high birth to me,
Richer than wealth, prouder than garments' costs,
Of more delight than bling and hearses be;
And having you, of all men's pride I boast:

Wretched in this alone, that Zak may take
All this away, and me most wretched make.

CXXXI

You are as tyrannous, so for your part,
As those whose beauties proudly make them cruel;
For well you know to my dear doting heart
You are the fairest and most precious jewel.
Yet, in good faith, some say since you've transformed,
Your face has not the power to make love groan;
To say they err I dare not be so bold,
Although I swear it to myself alone.
And to be sure that is not false I swear,
A thousand groans, but thinking on your face,
One on another's neck, do witness bear
Your pallor fairest in my judgment's place.
In nothing are you rank save in your deeds,
And thence this slander, as I think, proceeds.

CXXXVIII

When my love swears that she is made of truth,
I do believe her though I know she lies,
That she might think me some innocent youth,
Unchanged despite the world's mass casualties.
Thus vainly thinking she thinks me unstung,
Although she knows my days are past the best,
Simply I credit her false-speaking tongue:
On both sides thus is simple truth suppressed:
But wherefore says she not she is unjust?
And wherefore say not I that I molder?
O! love's best habit is in seeming trust,
And guilt in love, loves not to be free told:
Therefore, I ever lie, and after she,
And despite our faults we live happily.

XLIX

Against that time, if ever that time comes,
When I will see you snap at my defects,
When as your love has cast his utmost sums,
Called to that audit by viral infects;
Against that time when you shall strangely pass,
And fail to greet me with that sun, your eye,
When love, converted from the thing it was,
Shall seek my flesh with utmost gravity;
Against that time do I ensconce you here,
Within the knowledge of my own desert,
And this my hand, against myself uprear,
To guard the lovely reasons of your part:
To end poor me you have the strength of jaws,
Since for my love I can't enforce your pause.

7

Zombaby

His sole child, my lord... bequeathed to my overlooking. I have those hopes of her good that her education promises; her dispositions she inherits, which makes fair gifts fairer; for where an unclean mind carries virtuous qualities, there commendations go with pity-they are virtues and traitors too.... 'Tis the best brine a maiden can season her praise in. The remembrance of her father never approaches her heart but the tyranny of her sorrows takes all livelihood from her cheek.... If the living be enemy to the grief, the excess makes it soon mortal.—Countess of Rousillon, *All's Well That Ends Well* (I.1)

The drive to reproduce, to give birth to the sweet fruit of love, presses. It is the most human need, perhaps the only basic need that consumes all living things. Yet the simplicity betrays grandiosity. I remember the day you were born, my son. Called home from the theater, I knew I wasn't ready. And then I held you in my arms and the whole world changed. Your purple skin shone forth like the dawning sun into a dark world. Your tiny ears seemed as thin as parchment. Every tiny toe and grasping little finger held my heart. You awed me. I knew that somehow I was in the presence of a miracle.

The day that you passed is hardly less precious to me. Oh, Hamnet! My only son! How your loss haunts me. This cup of misery I would not have wished upon any—even the lowest, most defiled scourge on earth. Yet grateful am I that you passed at the earliest beginning of this plague. I am ever torn. I lament the world as I knew it, when all three of you were my hopes.

> With a great heart heave away this storm;
> Commend these waters to those baby eyes
> That never saw the giant world enraged,
> Nor met with fortune other than at feasts,

Full of warm blood....
—Lewis, *King John* [V.2]

Exiting this world was your blessing, my son. To never have witnessed the dawn of apocalypse surely leaves your soul brighter for its unalloyed purity.

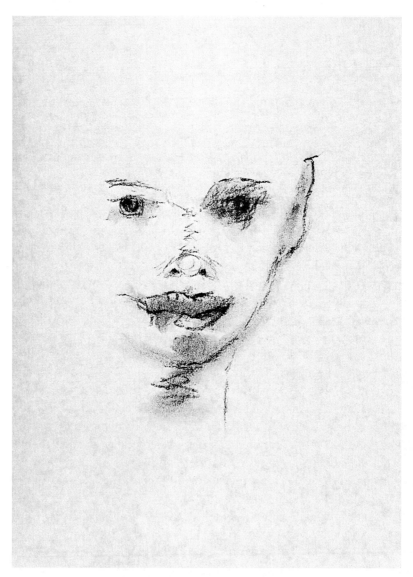

The guilt that runs like a river through my lucid consciousness reminds me that my days are spent bringing this horror to every other father alive. It is I who rob mothers of their futures, their precious hopes of survival; their daughters preserve instead my plague. Or, at best, both worlds survive—one in the visage, the other in the vessels. This plague carried with it the unsuspecting burden of eternity, eternally acting as its representative face, hovering over the face of the deep earth. I bring about the end and the beginning with each single taste. Each morsel alters the meal. We eat, together. We eat each other. Gloriously. Overcome with shame. Flesh torn.

And you, my daughter. My Judith. Life was complete when you were born. I'd achieved the dream. And even so, it was only beginning. The passion that you bring—even still—to everything, from combing your hair to telling stories, is boundless. Every breath you take fills the world with some joy that hadn't been before. And when you turned: somehow the gleam in your eye never left. Again your skin was paled. Your punctured calf was so irreal—how could it have even happened? It was the only exposed area on your whole body, save your beautiful little face. I suppose I should be grateful you weren't bitten on the nose. Would that you had been able to say what happened. And to think that I had been saving that moment for a special day. Only six days before your birthday it was. Such a robbery. Still you are yet as you as I am I. Vigorous. Strong. Fast. Verdant. Passionate.

> Unconditioned, diminutive monster;
> Ever-excess.
> Pathologically, beautifully enthusiastic:
> From the first,
> Unspeakable;
> Fairy-told dramatist,
> Unprovoked:
> Human hornet, driven to fly
> In ceaseless bursts through the hive:
> Into the chambers.
> In wisdom she knows,
> Boundless, critical, logical:
> With pleasure, perhaps,
> And passion's breath.

You are the record of zombie immortality no less than you were the recording of human eternity. In you the zeeds of immortality grew then even as now. The popular myth runs rampant: that the only way to witness a zombie birth is when a mother is infected while pregnant. No! It is not so. Zombies reproduce as potently as rabbits. The disease—contrary to the popular fallacy—infects the reproductive organs first. Better than oysters, more rigid than a codpiece, more receptive than springtime soil, the disease seeks to procreate above all else. In every way possible.

> And at that time he got his wife with child.
> Dead though she be, she feels her young one kick;
> So there's my riddle: one that's dead is quick—
> And now behold the meaning.
> —Diana, *All's Well That Ends Well* [V.3]

With good reason. Zombie babies are the most precious creatures on earth. Have you seen them crawling? Heard them calling? Drawn instinctively, groans distinctly blend with newborn cries. The pitch perfectly simultaneously instills fear in the living and endears the no-longer. In my best moments, you bring me comfort. Sweet, growing in confidence, negotiating the terrors and joys of the world— lucky to exist. Spirit carries them forward.

We mustn't, therefore, fail to breed zombie children. Memorial fixities in time, they will be the ones to preserve the lost. They will resist the grave decay that otherwise infects our species. They are the hope for the future. Oh Hamnet! Oh my Elizabeth! I mourn your loss, though you yet live. You were taken from me before I could even get the chance to know you by this awful disease. This awing disease. This tearing disease. Children in an infected world are the arbiters of hope—without your hope, all that is left is to mourn this horrible shadow. Ever. Yet ever remembering. I am of two souls, two minds. One zombie, one human. One condemned to die. One condemned to exist, tearing the flesh from the still bloody stump of humanity. Zombie babies, therefore, represent the hope of consummation. In them the world will be healed. There is no need to selfishly abstain from feeding nor from reproducing. The future is inevitable. It is for each to give up herself and himself to become the vessel of eternity on earth. Take courage, reader. Give yourself up to zombification. Go forth and multiply.

VII

Lo! in the orient when the gracious blight
Lifts up its burning head, each infectee
Does homage to his newfound appetite,
Serving with bites a sacred majesty;
And having climbed the steep-up heavenly hill,
Resembling strong youth in his middle age,
Immortal looks adore his beauty still,
Attending on his pied pilgrimage:
But when from highest vantage, food seems far,
Like feeble age, he reels wasting away...
The eyes, still hungry, now diverted are
From his low taste, and look another way:
To you, yourself fast fading in your noon:
Aging, forgot, unless you breed a son.

IX

Is it for fear to wet a widow's eye,
That you condemn yourself to single life?
Ah! if you issueless happen to die,
The world will wail you like a forlorn wife;
The world will be your widow and still weep
That you no form of you have left behind,
When every private widow well may keep
By children's eyes, her husband's shape in mind:
Look! Even ugly apocalyptic
Survivors are well worth a second date
But beauty's waste doubles that which is sick
Leaving the world without a lovely mate.
No love toward others in that bosom sits
That on himself such murderous shame commits.

XIII

O! that you were yourself; but, love, you are
No longer yours, than you your self here live:

Against this coming end you should prepare,
And your sweetest guts to some other give:
So should that beauty which you hold in lease
Find no awful grave ending; then you were
Yourself again, after yourself's decease,
When your sweet issue your sweet form should bear.
Who lets so fair a house fall to decay,
Which protection in honour might uphold,
Against the stormy gusts of winter's day
And barren rage of death's eternal cold?
O! none but unthrifts. Dear mother, you know,
Your life was good: now let your son turn you.

III

Look in your glass and tell the face you view
Now is the time that face should eat another;
Whose fresh repair if now you not renew,
You beguile the world, unbless some mother.
For where is she so fair whose unreared womb
Disdains the tillage of your husbandry?
Or who is he so fond will be the tomb,
Of his self-love to stop posterity?
You are your mother's spawn and she in you
Calls from your lovely inside go and eat;
So we proceed from house to house we knew,
Despite of bullets threatening our retreat.
Cuz if you live, remembered not to be,
Die hungry and your image dies surely.

XVII

Who will believe my verse in time to come,
If it were filled with your most base exploits?
Though yet heaven knows it is but a tomb
Which hides your life, and shows o'er half your guts.

If I could write the flatness of your eyes,
And in fresh numbers number your disgraces,
The age to come would say "This poet lies;
Such unholy touches never touched earthly faces."
So should my papers, yellowed like your ribcage,
Be scorned, like old men of less truth than tongue,
And your true rights be termed a poet's rage
And stretched meter of an antique song:
But were some victim of yours alive that time,
You should live thrice, in it, and in my rhyme.

XXXII

If you'd survived my pox infected days,
When grizzly Death my bones with dust will cover
And you by fortune once more appraised
These poor shaped lines of your deceased lover,
Compare them with those bettered by more time,
And though they're weak compared to every pen,
Reserve them for my love, not for their rhyme,
Exceeded by the height of happier men.
O! then leave to me this one loving thought:
"Had you, my muse, grown with this growing age,
A dearer birth than this, this love had brought,
To march in ranks of death's worse equipage:
But since you turned and better poets piled
Their style saved in this, this alone our child."

CXXIV

If my dear love's child could ever be sate,
It might, disease's bastard, unfathered,
Be subject to Time's love or to Time's hate,
Weeds among weeds, or flowers with flowers gathered.
No, it was built up far from accident;
It suffers not in smiling pomp, nor falls

Under the blow of angry discontent,
To the inviting time our fashion calls:
It fears not policy, that heretic,
Which works on leases of short-numbered hours,
But all alone stands hugely politic,
That it nor grows with food, nor drowns with showers.
To witness I call the fools of time's end,
Who die for innocence, who for state lived.

CXLIII

Lo, as a hungry housewife runs to catch
One of her sighted creatures broke-away,
Ignores her babe, and makes all swift dispatch
To pursue what would her hunger satisfy.
While her neglected child holds her in chase,
Cries to catch her whose busy care is bent
To follow that which flies before her face,
Not prizing her poor infant's discontent;
So you run after that which flies from you,
While I your babe chase you afar behind;
But if you catch your prey, turn back to me,
And play the mother's part, kiss me, be kind;
So will I pray that you may have your "Will,"
If you turn back and my loud groaning still.

8

Survivors

Proteus:
I grant, sweet love, that I did love a lady;
But she is dead.

Julia:
'Twere false, if I should speak it;
For I am sure she is not buried.
—*The Two Gentlemen of Verona* (IV.2)

What if you survived? This question haunts me every day. Would that it were not so. Where is the subtlety in it? The hope that it represents is twofold, both inevitably bankrupt. The question itself, first, suggests that I might have mattered to begin with had I survived, that perhaps somehow the world is better for my having persisted in it. And most days I think that probably I do make the world a little brighter. I invite the world to explore. To pretend as if all the world is a stage and I bring it about for them to ponder, briefly, as they roll around in the grass outside the monotony of the everyday of their lives. For a moment the filth recedes. For a moment the gilt all around frames their own portraits. The world, if not better, allows even the groundling to behave as if it was. I am the muse who sets fire to the imagination; I imagine a world more beautiful and bring it to life. Suppose within this text that shamblers come alive, foremost of them all, perhaps, me. And then my darling love. Only you, and the world might make sense again. All the words that I have ever written could be worth their salt if you, you only, were around to hear them. This is my daily ache.

Or worse, what if you didn't? You are undead. How can one give answer when one's lover postdates him? Or the very hope of his days, his child?

> What, dead, my dove?
> O Pyramus, arise,
> Speak, speak.
> —Thisby, *A Midsummer Night's Dream* [V.1]

If no answer can come save moaning, all is lost. Hope arises alongside the empty grave. Would that the survivor could resurrect their love. The widow witnessing the slow demise of her longtime husband: who would not choose to save him after all? The choice to reinvigorate the empty house, resonant with silence, is no choice at all. Even were joy to persist in memory only, the persistence of togetherness is too strong a drug to resist. No hand could stay its reach. No grasp self-chastise. No matter the cost. Wake up, my love. Wake up.

Or what if you were to be gone and the one who you loved were to survive you? Have you imagined such a thing? There is guilt in surviving. To postdate one's own world and all who populate it is the gravest tragedy of all. When the pencil line of my beard is marred by gore there will be no guilt. But until then, I survive, when all those I love simply persist. I am full. The anemic blue of your eyes has slowly faded day by day. The skin that was once so rich-hued has faded toward gray. It now hangs in tiny decaying rivulets, folds decrying the absence of whatever flesh had filled your clothes before. Would that even clothes would have remained in such repair. That the theater is full of hand-me-downs is no surprise to any; that all the world's tattered garments now crawl unfettered with lice and carrion feeding vermin ... ever surprises. Lady's dresses, farthingales, allow so much room for rodents that, without trapping, they breathe and spin and whirl by themselves. Before ever seeing her face, a zombie gentlewomen announces her presence by a loud squeaking from beneath her caned bodice. Yet somehow, I persist.

I awoke on that first frightening morning knowing that all was lost. The waking itself made me physically sick. For the first time I could feel the fractures in my soul. The gaps bled sorrow. The image of his little face, incomparable, precious, singular, appeared as a ghost over my every sight. The crushing weight of grief was more than I could bear. I sank back into my feathered mattress: perhaps it would drown me in a sea of feathers.

My chest constricts at the brightness of the brooding world, contrasting the sorrow of loss. I remember her, before. Simple joy. Held breath. Weighty within my body, pressing on my heart. Tears well unbidden and one out-of-place lock takes me back again to that first day. The day when her cheek blushed and turned underneath, the focal point of forever in a cacophony of voices. When the one that you have loved has passed, when your children are gone, there seems to be so little reason to live. Then when one looks outside, sees the sunset over the balcony or the dog lying with its pup, there returns beauty to the world. Its worth, the worth of the everyday, remains. In remains, survive. Tattered. Survive.

And perhaps every world is just the same. Stretching out toward the infinite, altering the lives of those around them irreparably and toward eternity. Far be it from me to lift the veil that separates the love and lives that each builds with each. On my best days I know that I matter. Even bitten I persist. If my writing succumbs, if my very body succumbs, it will have been a good existence.

When the days are brightest, I survive in the remembrance of the moments spent in each-other's company. It is a strange feeling, Ophelia, to know that there is hopelessness in the genesis of hope. When hope becomes possible it must acknowledge the inevitability of hopelessness, I suppose, an impossible perhaps breaking dawn into the day, admitting forever night to come. The emptying of the self is implicit in its constitution. Your life plays out, ever repeating in the joy and horror that somehow comprise the substance of my own survival. That I caused the end is too much to imagine, too painful to admit to myself. There is no forgetting, nor is there a mistaking of what was. Connection, soul-rending togethering, indissoluble, echoes in the pallid timbre of your voice. We survive. Flesh become one, one, because only one remains. How wrong you were when you supposed the possibility of forgetting.

Would that I had known before how much of my self would survive the transition. That self might persist in undeath is the greatest surprise of all.

XLI

Those pretty wrongs that apocalypse fit,
When I am sometime absent from your eyes,
Your hunger, and your tears full well show it,
For still temptation follows when you cry.

Tender you are, and therefore ripe for food,
Beautiful you are, therefore to be assailed;
And when a zombie coos, what sweet child's good
Will sourly leave her till he have prevailed?
Ay me! but yet you might warning beware,
And chide your beauty and your wandering youth,
Which lead you in their riot even there
Where you are forced to break a twofold truth:—
Beloved, you're safer sad in our lair,
Than in a zombie's false arms anywhere.

VIII

Dear one, why do you hear music sadly?
Sweets with sweets don't war, joy delights in joy:
Why take that which you received not gladly,
Or else receive with pleasure your annoy?
If the true concord of well-tuned sounds,
By unions married, harsh offends your ear,
They do but sweetly chide you, who confounds
In singleness the parts that you should bear.
Mark how one string, sweet husband to another,
Strikes each in each by mutual ordering;
Resembling dad and child and happy mother,
Who, all in one, one pleasing note do sing:
Whose speechless song being many, seems one,
Sings this to you: "Alone you will be done."

XLVIII

How careful I was when I went my way,
Each trifle within strong vaults to conceal,
That for my use each might unused stay
From infected hands, in sure safes of steel!
But you, next to whom my prizes ants are,
Most worthy comfort, now my greatest grief,

You, best and dearest, and my only care,
Are left the prey of every hungry thief.
You I have not locked up in any chest,
Save where you're not, and I pray never are,
Within the gentle closure of my breast,
From whence you may not unbecome my part.
And from there you won't be stolen I fear,
For none could steal a prize become so dear.

XV

When I consider every thing that grows
Holds in perfection but a little moment,
That this huge stage presents nothing but shows
Whereon the stars in secret influence comment;
When I perceive that men as plants increase,
Cheered and checked even by the self-same sky,
Turgid in youthful sap, at height decrease,
And wear their brave state out of memory;
Then the conceit of this inconstant stay
Sets you most rich in youth before my sight,
Where wasteful plague debates with decay
To change your day of youth to sullied night,
And all in war with Zak for love of you,
As he reaches for you, I pick you anew.

XXV

Let those who are in favor with their stars
Of public honor and proud titles boast,
While I, whom fortune of such triumph bars
Unlooked for joy in what I honor most.
The prettiest models their fair leaves spread
But as the marigold at the sun's eye,
And in themselves their pride lies buried,
For with a wound they in their glory die.

The painful warrior famous for fight,
After a thousand head shots just once foiled,
Is from the book of honor erased quite,
And all the rest forgot for which he toiled:
Then happy I, that love and am beloved,
Proved victorious even at world's end.

LV

Not marble, nor the gilded monuments
Of princes, shall outlive this apocalypse;
Though you shall shine more bright in these contents
Than brightest red, besmeared on sluttish lips.
When wasteful war shall statues overturn,
And broils root out the work of masonry,
Nor Mars his sword, nor war's quick fire shall burn
The living record of your memory.
Against death, and oblivious enmity
Shall you pace forth; your praise shall still find room
Even in the eyes of all posterity
That wear this world out to the ending doom.
So, till judgment of the world is complete
You live in this, and dwell within my heart.

LVII

Being your slave what should I do but tend,
Upon the hours, and times of your desire?
I have no precious time at all to spend;
Nor services to do, till you require.
Nor dare I chide that one world-ending hour,
That knit, my sovereign, our futures to rot,
Nor think the bitterness of absence sour,
When you have loosed your servant from thought;
Nor dare I question with my jealous mind
Where you may be, or your affairs suppose,

But, like a sad slave, stay and think you kind
And, where you are, how happy you make those.
So true a fool is love, that in your will,
Though you do anything, he thinks no ill.

LXXXVIII

When you determine to set me alight,
And place my body in the blaze of scorn,
Upon your side, against myself I'll fight,
And prove your virtue, though I am forsworn.
With my own weakness, being best acquainted,
Upon your part I can set down a story
Of friends digested, with whom I'm tainted;
That you in losing me shall win much safety:
And I by this will be a gainer too;
For bending all my loving thoughts on you,
I risk both of our lives, I know it's true
Imperiling our whole group, even you.
Such is my love, to you I so belong,
That to save your life, I will bear the throng.

CXL

Be wise as you drip rancid drool; don't press
My naked skull for too much of my brain,
Lest the loss end our world, and words express
The manner of my pity-wanting pain.
If I aid your undeath, better it were,
Though not to love, yet, love to tell me so;—
As testy sick men, when their deaths be near,
No news but health from their physicians know;—
For, if I should despair, I should grow mad,
And in my madness might for you seek ill;
Now this ill-wresting world is grown so bad,
Mad slanderers with mad minds seek to kill.

That I may not be so, nor you belied,
Leave my brain whole, though my proud heart eat fried.

CXLIX

Can you, O cruel! Say I love you not,
When I against myself with you partake?
Do I not think on you, when I forget
All of myself, my tyrant, for your sake?
Who hates your kind that I still call my friend,
On whom do you frown that I fawn upon?
No! If you lower upon me, do I not spend
Revenge upon myself with present moan?
What merit do I in myself respect,
That is so proud your service to despise,
When all my best worships your sad defect,
Commanded by the motion of your eyes?
But, love, hate on, for now I know your mind;
All those can see you've turned, and I am blind.

9

Don't Die Yet

I here importune death awhile, until
Of many thousand kisses the poor last
I lay upon thy lips.
—Antony, *The Tragedy of Antony and Cleopatra* (IV.15)

It is the unsettling vacancy in her eyes that pricks me this time as I watch her sleep. They are open but she is eerily absent. From vibrant new love to wilting botanist, she has transformed, and will continue. And again I see a tiny army of carapace-wearing shamblers hustle forward and past, walking into a mirror of themselves—dimmer each day than the last. But for the one, unawares, she walks on, instead an actor in her own destiny. She chose to become, to be. She has joined us.

I hold the icy grasp of death at bay forever so that I may make known myself before I rot into oblivion. Its shadow looms ever present, clinging to my very being. I can never be gone.

Holding with an iron fist to the pale fragile bloom of a rose inevitably crushes the essence of its beauty. Too tenuous is its lease. So I must beg pause, Gertrude. Hold for one moment yet though your skin has grown taut and your neck rigid with fright. Surely it is not yet the effect of the disease that takes hold. Pierce me no longer with your blank stare. Let not your blackened eyes haunt me to infinity. Rather leave me with memories unclogged...

I called them snowball trees when I was a little boy. They made up the hedgerow nearest my cottage in Stratford-upon-Avon and dotted the garden. How I cherish the days I spent wandering through the garden and overlooking it from the upstairs window. I can still remember looking out in the twilight, thick fog glistening in the air illuminated by the sun's dimmer cousin. Those days were simpler. It was enough to live in the easy beauty of the world. As the last snowball bounced in the breeze, my mind wandered forward and back, ever toward the future and what I might be and anon toward the warmth of the fire and my mother's arms. It seems that those days can't last; they must inevitably give way to the cares of the world—to profit, status, legacy. And how much more now does that last snowball still bobble in the wind, fixed in my mind, symbol of

gamboling days and worry-free, hopeful nights. They are the symbols of hope. Already browned with age, they mustn't die. Hope must not yet die.

And again I think of you, my love, and need for you to yet stay as you were. You are a fixity in my mind. You must be. The moments I've spent with you live outside time, frozen forever in my memory. The day when you wore your new dress for the first time—blazing white—tiny fibers softening your frame, and it caught afternoon sunlight through the open window framing the joy on your face: that day yet lives. Your hair brushing my face when you held me for the first time still grazes my cheek. The hesitancy as you reached for my hand for the first time and my own as I reached to meet yours lives. That ridiculous minstrel singing of kids in trouble and silver cities and silver girls echoes. You did not eat my brains. I did not eat your brains. Years and years cannot die in a day. No, they must not. Our experiences aren't complete when they happen, they live and live. The almost tangible memories become full over the course of our lives, turned over like wagon wheels, always steering us as we move forward. I cling to the hope that your fair snowy dress and my own spent hydrangeas mustn't die. Not yet.

Disfigured by the day, defaced memory fades from my mind, parchment left too-long in the sun. Withered and weathered, tinged with gore, my mind mirrors your face. And yet even so, ever so, I hope. I hope against the last kiss that must surely come. The world survives in the paired visages of Janus, equally toward the future and mired in the past. Zombie and human share the same body, the same streets, the same brains. I desire nothing more than your turning. I desire nothing more than the last human kiss before you do. In that single kiss rests the whole of heaven and earth. In it is hope for the turned future. In it is the warmth of the human, your lips being used as they were made before finding themselves *rouge sang*, blood red. Is it your lips that I mourn in advance? Or is it my own future, already fled?

The flexing muscles in your cheeks, warm and vivacious, still occupy my mind. Dimples form and vanish. Pale blush blooms, dawn's visitant. Graceful fingers remain innocent, colored only by the art of our minds, not the gore of our innards. Each tiny bite, carefully-chosen, speaks of your self-control. Hair falls in wisps across your shoulders; no need of plaster betrays itself. I see the glistening in your eyes, dear Juliet, spangling the day with jealousy. Can I say that the cling of your bodice sets fire even to the undead? It is with unreflected glory and hunger that I see you.

> Howl, howl, howl, howl! O, you are men of stone.
> Had I your tongues and eyes, I'd use them so
> That heaven's vault should crack. She's gone for ever!
> I know when one is dead, and when one lives.
> She's dead as earth.
> —Lear, *The Tragedy of King Lear* [V.3]

When you learned that men were all undone you simply saw too much. Each heart carries forth nothing more than longing and craving. It is the zombie that wears his heart on his sleeve. It is the zombie who is honest. You had to learn that truth threatens tragedy, my dear love. Yet there could have been no other way. The heart of man is hard and dark. Yet now that the world is honest, we can live together; we can love together. We will never have the wall of life between us again. We have become one in the flesh.

LXI

> Is it your will that your image keep open
> My heavy eyelids in the weary night?
> Do you desire my slumbers should be broken,
> While you-shaped gruesome shadows mock my sight?
> Is it your spirit that you've sent to me
> So far from home into my deeds to pry,
> To find out shames and weakness in me,
> The scope and tenure of your jealousy?
> O, no! your love, though much, is not so great:
> It is my love that keeps my eyes awake:
> My own true love that makes my rest defeat,
> To play the watchman ever for your sake:
> For you I watch, while you awake elsewhere,
> From me far off, with zombies all too near.

XIV

Not from space do I my dark judgement pluck;
And yet I think I know astronomy,
But not to tell of good or evil luck,
Of plagues, of deaths, or seasons' quality;
Nor can I fortunes in brief minutes tell,
Pointing to each his thunder, rain, and wind,
Or say with lovers if it shall go well
Or whether from hell, haven you will find.
But from your eyes, my knowledge I derive,
By constant stars in them I read the chart:
See truth and beauty together survive,
And all will be well if we never part.
Or else of you this I prognosticate:
Your end is truth's and beauty's doom and date.

XXI

It is not for me your sight to abuse,
Stirred by a painted beauty to this verse,
Who heaven itself for ornament makes use
And every fair with his fair doth rehearse,
Crafting a couplement of proud compare
With sun and moon, with earth and sea's rich gems,
With April's first-born flowers, and all things rare,
That heaven's air in this huge rondure hems.
O! let me, true in love, but truly write,
This plague has left you as wounded and scarred
As any syphilitic child; though blight
Left you alive and outside badly marred,
Your graceful moves and deadly skill rival
Only my resolution to survive.

XXIII

As an imperfect actor on the stage,
Who with his fear is put beside his role,

Or some fierce Z replete with too much rage,
Whose strength's abundance tears his own muscle;
So I, for fear of dismemberment, hush
The perfect ceremony of love's rite,
And in my own love's strength decay to mush,
Overcharged with burden of my own love's might.
O! let my looks be then the eloquence
And dumb foreshadows of my speaking breast,
Who plead for love, from safety's safe silence,
More than that tongue that more has more expressed.
O! learn to read what silent love's spoken:
To hear with eyes is safe love's fine token.

X

For shame! deny you bear love to any,
Who for you offer squat, unprovident.
Grant, if you will, you are loved by many,
But that you none love is most evident:
For you are so possessed with murderous hate,
That against yourself you seek not to conspire,
Seeking that beauteous spouse to ruinate
Which to repair should be your chief desire.
O! change your thought, that I may change my mind:
Shall hate be fairer lodged than gentle love?
Be, as your presence is, gracious and kind,
Or to yourself at least kind-hearted prove:
Infect another self for love of me,
That beauty still may live in yours or you.

XXXVII

As a decrepit father takes delight
To see his active child do feats of youth,
So I, made lame by amputation's blight,
Take all my comfort from your worth and truth;

For whether beauty, birth, or wealth, or wit,
Or any of these all, or all, or more,
Entitled in all your parts, crowned sit,
I graft my incomplete love to this store:
So then I am not lame, poor, nor despised,
While that your shadow does such substance give
That I in your abundance am completed,
And by a part of all your glory live.
Look what is best, that best I wish to be:
This wish I have—you live! My self complete.

XXXIX

O! how your worth with manners may I sing,
When you are all the better part of me?
What can my own praise to my trapped self bring?
And what else might I praise save this body?
Even for this, let us divided live,
My dear teeth chatter apart from this mind,
That by this separation I may give
That due to you which you deserve alone.
O carnage! what a torment you would prove,
If this body would only have leisure
To entertain wants without thoughts above,
Eating more than one could ever measure.
And so I would for nothing make us twain,
Praising him here who would weakly remain.

LXXXVII

Farewell! You are too dear for my possessing,
And like enough you know your estimate,
The measure of your worth gives you releasing;
As you lay here gurgling for a moment.
For how could I survive without your gift?
And how could I repay your sacrifice?

For me you took the bite that would have rift
My subject on this earth from its sentence.
Your self you gave, your worth then not knowing,
Or me to whom you gave it, else mistaking
Your real value for my gilded showing,
Debiting the earth and poorer making.
Thus have I been rich, as a dream does flatter,
In sleep a king, but waking no such matter.

XCVI

Some say your fault is appetite, some bite;
Some say you've lost youth's grace and gentle sport;
Both grace and faults are loved of more and less:
You make faults graces my lovely consort.
As on the finger of an enthroned queen
The basest jewel will be well esteemed,
So are those errors that in you are seen
To truths translated, and for true things deemed.
How many lambs would the stern wolf betray,
If with sheep's clothes he could his looks translate!
How many walkers might you lead astray,
If you would use the strength of your grave state!
But do not so; I love you in such sort,
For, being mine, you save me from your sport.

CXXIX

The expense of spirit in a waste of shame
Is cannibalism: and till action, biting
Is perjured, murderous, bloody, full of blame,
Savage, extreme, rude, cruel, unsightly;
Enjoyed no sooner but despised straight;
Past reason hunted; and no sooner had,
Past reason hated, as a swallowed bait,
On purpose laid to make the taker mad:

Mad in pursuit and in possession so;
Had, having, and in quest, to have extreme;
A bliss in proof,— and proved, a very woe;
Before, a joy proposed; behind a dream.
All this the world well knows; yet none knows well
To shun the flesh that leads men to this hell.

CXLVI

Poor soul, the center of my sinful earth,
My sinful earth these rebel powers array,
Why do you pine within and suffer dearth,
Panting with outward tongue so ghastly gray?
Why so large cost, having so short a lease,
Do you upon your fading mansion spend?
Shall worms, inheritors of this excess,
Eat up your charge? Is this your body's end?
Then soul, live upon your servant's less,
And let that pine to vast increase your store;
Starve to nourish rather than eat friends best;
Within be fed, without be rich no more:
So shall you feed on Death, that feeds on men,
And Death once dead, there's no more dying then.

10

Epitaph

This grave shall have a living monument.
—Claudius, *Hamlet* (V.1)

It is in the epitaph that the paradox of memory crystalizes. Fully half the graves in this lustrum feature nothing more than empty words adorning empty maws. To what end? There seems to be no reason to bother with memorializing walkers. They live in undeath. Markers of their decease are entirely superfluous except as vestiges of a time when bodies moldered beneath the surface rather than above it.

Epitaphs exist for the living—to help them remember the dead. There are now neither living nor dead, always ever only both. They answer the question, "who lies here?" Yet there is never the sense that the whole of the person is captured in even the longest of epitaphs. If the living write the epitaph, it remembers none but the writer. If the dead, none but the painted face of the corpse, perhaps none at all. Even my own epitaph, a living monument, records not the person I was nor the thing I have become. It lives alongside me, a monster of my own creation.

Yet perhaps epitaphs exist for the dead to help them remain alive. Ever and ever I preserve here in these words. I bring to life those already dead. I preserve them as figures in jars calling out to be seen and beloved. I give them persistence despite the putrefying state in which they now find themselves. Would that I could preserve the sight of a morning as rain breaks over the countryside. Spring blossoms on apple trees and meadows fully green with new growth floor and wall the scene, infinite heavens open vast the vault.

There is all the more reason to remember the beauty of the soul now, before everything started to fall apart. The purpose of all figurative language is to bring life to the dead. They are literally figured in each of these letters in perhaps the only way that they can be. Now. So grave words are for the undead—framing bodily structure day by day unchanged even as chartreuse deepens toward moss. Why must we remember? What is the point in infinitely archiving the beauty and the tragedy of this life? It is this archive that shapes the soul to be memorialized to be sure. There is indeed a point to memorializing in verse the life of one who we have loved.

The alleviation of the fear that we might utterly erase from the earth is among the chief ends of writing. The erasure of this fear makes existence deplorable. Its very infinity stretches out toward the darkest space threatening rather than promising forever.

Perhaps life cannot have been meaningful if we are to be forgotten at the end of our lives. It certainly cannot be meaningful if it continues ad nauseum. If, when we have passed, the self that we knew is gone, then the hair's breadth sliver that we have occupied is of no worth. If breath stretches to eternity there is no responsibility. We will have had no meaning. There is salve in this collection of epitaphs. And yet it is not about remembering the one departed, even so. The writing is about inspiring in the reader something that continues to matter. There is no hope of memorializing the one become zombie as that one was. They are indeed no longer the same self, and further, they persist as a new self. Impossible become possible.

The memorialization of the self is a creation of meaning, therefore, and not a recording of meaning that was already present.

We are elevated by sacred principles—of the meaning of the individual, of the right to persist—and we, therefore, inspire each other to greatness in the quest to preserve the intricacies of memory and the selves that lay submerged beneath the archive.

Yet even so, how can I ever hope to preserve the way that the light broke over Juliet's face that day on the balcony? The play of light on her skin lives in my mind, forever shaping me and my feelings for her, even as they indelibly expanded my map of beauty. How can I preserve the tender caress on my face? How can I preserve the sound of my son's laughter at 3 and at 6 years old? Do you remember, reader,

when she or he, your own beloved child, wondered about growir
Before they were too far along already to see the boundaries of t
world carved for them? Can you still feel Cordelia's innocent lov
do, yet, when I can pause long enough to step forth from the ma
time. That is what I choose to memorialize. Each of those mome
that shape us. And yet I know as well that they will, that they ha
already passed on in the moment when I turned. That you will o

read these words and imagine the sweet laughter of your own little love, whether or not she or he has already grown. Would that you could for a moment remember when my boy blessed "the whole God" in his innocent prayer. Impossible. Would that you could remember the words of your own little love.

Shadows overtake the day and corruption marks the dissolution of life as we have known it. Lovers that went wrong. Loves that went awry. Moments that were supposed to last forever, youth that was to last until forever, the very hopes of this generation: all have been laid waste. The dead somehow manage to speak from beyond the grave. Our feelings, already dead, refuse to die. This is the apocalyptic irony: the face of the lifeless, long since slain from the hours of the everyday, will not die. It is forever fixed in memory, into the most precious spaces, the deepest recesses, from which the substance of life proceeds. Would that this memory would die alongside its bearer. But this, too, is out of reach.

Can you imagine, Oh reader!, living forever with the ghost of the one gone? That is pure madness. Surely every turn toward her will be the last, every hoped-for whisper unspoken the last specter to haunt this troubled mind. The truth is that some days surprise with utter joy; others are pocked with abject misery and a sense of loss so profound that there aren't words to express it.

CVII

Not my own fears, nor the prophetic soul
Of the wide world dreaming on things to come,
Can extend the lease of living control,
Supposed as forfeit to a confined doom.
The mortal moon has her eclipse endured,
And the astrologers mock their own days;
Uncertainties now crown themselves assured,
And peace proclaims olives of endless age.
Now with the drops of this most balmy time,
My life looks fresh! Death to me surrenders,
Since, spite of him, I'll live in this poor rime,
Untouched while plague overtakes, horrendous:

And you in this will find my monument,
When others' fleet moments are fully spent.

CXXII

Your gift, your tables, are within my brain
Full charactered with lasting memory,
Which shall above my idle, rank remains,
Beyond all date; even to eternity:
Or, at the least, so long as flesh and heart
Have faculty by nature to subsist;
Till each to razed oblivion yield his part
Of you, your record never can be missed.
That poor retention could not so much hold,
Nor need I tallies your dear love to score;
Therefore to give them from me was I bold,
To trust those tables that receive you more:
To remember by keeping a relic
Imports forgetfulness to my stomach.

XVIII

Shall I compare you to a summer's day?
You are less alive and more violent:
Sleepy afternoons waste the days of May,
And summer's lease has all too short a date:
Sometime too hot the eye of heaven shines,
And often comes the scratch from nails untrimmed,
And every fair from life sometime declines,
By bite, or nature's changing course unstemmed:
But your eternal summer will not fade,
Nor lose possession of that thrill you own,
Nor shall death brag you wander in his shade,
When in eternal undeath you return:
So long as men can breathe, or eyes can see,
So long lives this, an epitaph to thee.

XXIV

My eye has played the painter and pictured
Your beauty's form on canvas in my heart;
My mind the gallery where it's featured
And it is doubtless this painter's best art.
For through the painter must you see his skill,
To find where true momento mori lies,
Which in my bosom's shop is hanging still,
That has his windows glazed with your eyes.
Now see what good turns eyes for eyes have done:
My eyes have drawn your shape, as if alive
Like windows to my breast, through which the sun
Delights to peep, to gaze on your archive;
Yet eyes this cunning want to grace their art,
They draw the seen, yet never know the heart.

XXX

When to the sessions of sweet silent thought
I summon up nostalgia for things passed,
I sigh the lack of many a one I sought,—
And with old woes new wail my dear time's waste:
Then can I drown an eye, unused to flow,
For precious friends hid in death's dateless night,
And weep afresh love's long since cancelled woe,
And moan the expense of many a vanished sight:
Then can I grieve at grievances foregone,
And heavily from woe to woe tell over
The sad account of fore-bemoaned moan,
Which I pay new as if not paid before.
But if the while I think of you, dear friend,
All losses are restored and sorrows end.

XLV

The other two, hunger, and utter fear
Are both with you, whenever you've gone;

The first my thought, the other my tear,
These present-absent in swift evening dawn.
For when these quicker elements are gone
In tender embassy of love from me,
My heart, being made of four, with two alone
Sinks down to death, oppressed with melancholy;
Until life's composition be recured
By those your messengers returned swiftly,
Who even but now come back again, assured,
Of your fair survival, recount to me:
This told, I joy; but then no longer glad,
I send them back again, and straight grow sad.

LXIII

For when my love shall be as I am now,
With Zak's injurious hand crushed and worn;
When Z's have drained his blood and filled his brow
With wounds and bite marks; when his youthful morn
Has travelled on to melancholy night;
And all those beauties whereof now he's king
Are vanishing, or vanished out of sight,
Stealing away the treasure of his spring;
For such a time do I now fortify
Against confounding virus' cruel knife,
That it shall never cut from memory
My sweet love's beauty, though my lover's life:
His beauty shall in these black lines be seen,
And they shall live, though he is undead-green.

LXV

Not brass, nor stone, nor earth, nor boundless sea,
But sad mortality oversways their power,
How with this rage shall beauty hold a plea,
Whose action is no stronger than a flower?

O! how shall summer's honey-breath hold out,
Against the wrackful siege of battering days,
When rocks impregnable are not so stout,
Nor gates of steel so strong before Decays?
O fearful meditation! where, alack,
Shall my best jewel from hungry jaws lie hid?
Or what strong hand can hold their swift feet back?
Or who their spoil of beauty can forbid?
O! none, unless this miracle have might,
That in black ink my love may still shine bright.

LXXIV

But be contented! when that sad arrest
Without all bail shall carry me away,
My life has in this line some interest,
Which for memorial still with you will stay.
When you reread these words, you yet review
The very part was consecrate to you:
Though my body's constrained to walk taboo
My spirit is yours, the better part your due:
So if then you have no grave to visit,
No prey for worms, no body in the ground;
You've lost the dregs of life, for you unfit
For even a moment's sad sorrow's sound.
While worthless body repeats its refrain
My soul's in this, and this with you remains.

LXXVII

Your glass will show you how your beauties wear,
Your watch how your precious minutes waste;
These vacant sheets your mind's imprint will bear,
And of this book, this learning might you taste.
The wrinkles which your glass will truly show
Of mouthed graves will give you memory;

You by your watch's shady stealth might know
Time's thievish progress to eternity.
Look! what your memory cannot contain,
Commit to these waste blanks, and you will find
Those children nursed, delivered from your brain,
To take a new acquaintance of your mind.
And what eternity cannot contain
Will walk this earth: this ink your soul retains.

LXXXI

Perhaps I'll live to write your epitaph,
Or you'll survive when I to earth fall rotten;
From hence your memory death cannot slash,
Although in me each part will be forgotten.
Your name from hence immortal life shall have,
Though I, once gone, to all the world must die:
And earth refuse me even common grave,
Then you entombed in hungry eyes shall lie.
Your monument shall be my gentle verse,
Which eyes not yet created shall close-read;
And tongues to be, your being shall rehearse,
When all unbreathers in this world are dead;
You still shall live, such virtue has my pen,
Where breath most breathes, even in the mouths of men.

11

The Horde

O proud Death,
What feast is toward in thine eternal cell
That thou so many princes at a shot
So bloodily hast struck.
—Fortinbras, *Hamlet* (V.2)

When a thousand arms reach for you, there can be no more lone-liness. The pride of undeath is not to be underestimated. We fly high the tattered flag of decay. We are one. Each of us has been seduced by the promise of continuing on, toward infinity and beyond. We no longer fear the icy grip of death. We no longer fear anything at all, in fact.

The most obvious advantage of participation in the horde is that together we leave fear behind. It no longer controls us. Once the sub-ject of so many pamphlets, the sower of so much discord, the very basis of our relationship with God, fear lives no more. What then is the question for a zombie god? What is the secret held in reserve if not life eternal? The erasure of fear leaves us with no sense that god might be waiting to smite us for our iniquities. We do not dangle from a spider's thread; nor do we wait breathless as the threat of light-ning pierces the storm cloud. The basis of relationship with the zom-bie god is resurrection, plain and secure. Then it is increase. We together are responsible for proliferation. We must proselytize. As the resurrected, we must atone for humanity. We may very well be the realization of heaven on earth.

Yes, this sounds like heresy. But these hungry times call for a new theology. God has always been the feeder of the hungry, always the

106

hand with control over the boundary between life and death, the end of sorrow. The zombie god is no different. There remains hope in this apocalypse, the storm not too sore to abash the dove. We look forward to the outcome as fervently as ever; the hope of church rings through every jaw's clinch.

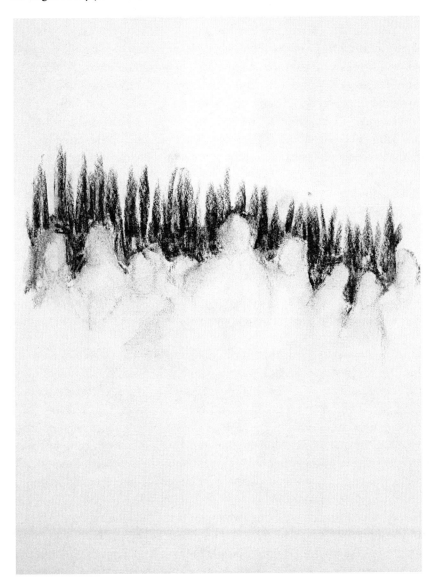

There is likewise no fear of an all-seeing and judging eye gazing from within the horde. That is the effect of real equality. My neighbors don't care a bit now whether or not I'm wearing pants of the season. My wig is long since musted in the corner. Thus the worst fear of all, the fear that we will not measure up, no longer weighs on this zombie heart. It's easy to pity those with the vestigial capacity to feel.

Together we can appreciate the sunset's pale hues, the pastel pinks blending to grey that blanket the hungry world. The silhouettes of barren trees stark before its softness reach toward each the same, comfort the weary in exactly the same way, hallmark days lived and days died in perfectly fairhanded means.

The mythic isolation supposed to infect members of the horde—the inability to speak and communicate—would be tragic. However, let me assure you, it is a false supposition. As you can see, very often, by and large we communicate nearly as well as we did before. The trade is quite worthwhile. There is, further, something gained in the trade that would not otherwise be: the living memorial carried on in the bodies of the horde. Each one of us is felt and heard. Always. What human can say the same? What group could ever approach the inclusivity of the zombie horde? None. No army, no culture, no government can give voice to all of its members. Not even a family could persist as effectively as we. Thus what is our monument toward eternity? Life, undeath, eternal, collaborative. In its way, on its own terms, it is beautiful.

What is perhaps most beautiful about the horde is its wake. In the aftermath of apocalypse, the time when the world as it was known has ended, all is new. The same must be true of the fire that destroys buildings of wood, even the Globe. It is in the rebuilding that the world can become new. In the wake of fire, new growth rises from the ashes. In the wake of the horde, the world itself becomes renewed. Each parting life leaves behind its worst and partakes with the rest of the new bread and wine, making a new covenant together. Together we remake a new kingdom.

What is more, we are beautifully honest. In no human gathering could all pretenses be dropped. We need not ever put on antic dispositions. There is no uncertainty that plagues us. Every one is equal in the horde. Blissfully, blessedly, of the same status and import. Confidence.

Surety. Inclusivity. This is the lot of the horde. "Feast the army!" cries Caesar in *The Tragedy of Antony and Cleopatra* (IV.1).

The gift of the horde is real, final unity. But do not despair: we have not degenerated toward equally sharing in the spoils with no real work. Each brings real value and is no longer isolated from their prey and the work to pursue it. We possess. Graciously. And we store in the very real sense the bodies of our prey in our flesh. Flesh for flesh.

The great equalizer makes certain within the hearts of all our kind the knowledge that each matters and that none may stand out. Even I am no more than one amongst the many.

Now to the extent that there is more sumptuous victual, each may yet aspire. There remains a critical sense of hope for the tastiest morsel. There is ever an urge onward. Together. Unled except by our own innards we hail only the light of day visible between the outstretched arms of another of our kind.

Together we are everything. Would that humans could live like we do—together. It has become completely clear that they cannot; it is up to us to renew the world. Selfishness so thoroughly debases human goodness. One rogue wolf can consume the whole flock. And they sometimes do. Then none can be eaten. What greater tragedy could there be than to lose them all, flesh and soul?

Every body given up to the horde pays dividends tenfold, exponentially increasing the sacrifice.

CXXV

It's naught to me to bear life's canopy,
With my extern the outward honoring,
Nor to craft monuments to eternity,
Which proves more short than waste or ruining.
Have I not seen vegetarians crave
Eating meat and more which with teeth they've rent
And counting sweet the gore, simple flavor
Of human brain for which their lives they've spent.
No; let me be innocent in your heart,
And please take my offering poor but free,

Which is not mixed with seconds, knows no art,
But mutual render, only you for me.
Here, my sweetest love! I give a true soul
Partake with me: let's abandon control.

XIX

Devouring horde, crunch flat the lion's paws,
And make the earth devour her own sweet brood;
Pluck the keen teeth from the fierce tiger's jaws,
And drown the long-lived phoenix in her blood;
Make hard and sorry seasons as you pass;
Do whatever you will, slow-footed bunch,
To the wide world and all her fading sweets;
But I forbid you one most heinous lunch:
O! carve not with your jaws my love's fair brow,
Nor scrape no wounds there with your gory nails;
Him in your course untainted do allow
For beauty's pattern: he must never fail.
Yet, do your worst undeath: despite your wrong,
My love shall in my verse ever live young.

LXXV

So are you to my thoughts as food to life,
Or as sweet-seasoned burger that's been ground;
And for the piece of you I hold, such strife
As between a miser and wealth is found.
Now proud to carve and show the herd a bone
Doubting the filching bunch will steal treasure;
Now counting best to feast on you alone,
Than bettered by their sight of my pleasure:
Sometime I'm full with gorging on your sight,
And by and by starved for a mouthful;
Possessing or pursuing no delight,
Save what is had, or must from you be pulled.

Thus do I pine and surfeit day by day,
Or gluttoning on all, or all away.

LXXVIII

So oft have I invoked you for my Muse,
And found such fair assistance in my verse
As every alien pen has got my use
And under you their poetry dispersed.
Your eyes, that taught the dumb on high to sing
And heavy ignorance aloft to fly,
Have added feathers to the learned's wing
And given grace a double majesty.
Yet be most proud of that which I compile,
Whose influence is yours, and born of you:
Others' works praise merit, though dead—alive
And arts with your sweet graces graced true;
But your memory is my art: rich, full
Filling the horde's stomach: insatiable.

CXXVIII

How oft when you, my lovely corpse, moans say,
From out of that blessed throat whose motion sounds
With your sweet lips when you most gently sway
Within the massive horde mine ear confounds,
Do I envy those jacks that nimble leap,
To nibble the tender inward of your hand,
Whilst my poor lips which should that harvest reap,
At the wound's blushing boldness by you stand!
To be so changed, they would trade their state
And situation with those dancing hips,
On whom your fingers claw with hope to sate,
Making dead flesh more blessed than living lips.
Since saucy jacks so happy are in waste,
Give them your fingers, me your lips to taste.

VI

Then let not rotten ragged hands deface,
In you your summer, ere you be distilled:
Make sweet some vial; treasure you some place
With beauty's treasure ere it be self-killed.
That use is not forbidden usury,
Which happys those that pay the willing loan;
For when you breed another you, to be
Now or ten times happier, ten for one,
Then, in horde, ten times you're made happier,
If ten of your ten times refigured be:
Then what could death do if you should depart,
Leaving you living in posterity?
Be not self-willed, for you are much too fair
To be death's conquest and make worms your heir.

CXXXVI

If your soul checks you that I come so near,
Swear to your blind soul that I'm still your "Will,"
And will, your soul knows, is admitted there;
Thus far for love, my love-suit, sweet, fulfill.
"Will," will fulfil the treasure of your love,
Ay, fill it full with wills, and my will one.
Despite seeming changes I still can prove
That my own will remains second to none.
Then in the number let me pass untold,
Though in your store's account I must be one;
For nothing halts me, no hint of mold
Grows in me, though I'm less than sweet to see.
Make but my name your love, and love that still,
And then you love me for my name's still "Will."

LXIX

Those parts of you that the world's eye can view
Need nothing that the thoughts of brains can't mend;

All tongues—the voice of souls—give you that due,
With bare truth, as enemies commend.
Your outward thus with outward praise is crowned;
But those same tongues, that give you so your own,
With other accents develop praise profound
By seeing farther than the eye has shown.
They sniff into the beauty of your mind,
And by tasting, measure based on your deeds;
Then—jerks—their thoughts, although their eyes were kind,
To your fair flower add the rank smell of weeds:
Because your garden's plants, gorgeous in show,
Fertilize from out flesh of those you know.

12

Grave Love

When the devout religion of mine eye
Maintains such falsehood, then turn tears to fires;
And these, who, often drown'd, could never die,
Transparent heretics, be burnt for liars!
One fairer than my love? The all-seeing sun
Ne'er saw her match since first the world begun.
—Romeo, *The Tragedy of Romeo and Juliet* (I.2)

There she sits, fair lady. Wearing her ring: brazen and bold. The hug they shared when she entered was more than enough to make the walls blush. She is well put-together; each hair gently maneuvered into place. He is dressed, quite obviously, as if he thought about every accoutrement, but sought to keep his careful thoughtfulness close to the vest. Freshly shaved face, sleeves rolled just so.... When she reached to pull her hair from his beard—and he reached to smooth a crumb from her blouse the candles brightened. Just for a moment, almost imperceptibly. A secreted present, drawn from its safe, squirreled-away pocket, sparkles in the light. It's silly: she laughs. He is her reflection. Ever so slightly sheer, her shirt, a choice, speaks her mind. Leaning toward each other their faces almost touch. Each breath mingles at that distance. Her smile is radiant; his too sly.

Her lip curls just so over the idea that she seems to be consider-ing. It isn't a full smile, just enough to flick the cat's-tail-corner of her mouth toward the sky. There is so much in that idea. So much behind it. Her mouth holds the hope for the future and peace for now, surely. Breathless, she moves amongst the tables. Serving up mostly to the imagination whatever it is that she has. Too sweet her portrait, so much obscured by framing flax. It's the crimson streak just below the

neckline that adds just enough crass to make this Beatrice palatable. Otherwise she could not live amongst this world.

The glance in her eyes betrays her, though she seems not to realize. Innocent but magnetic, it is curiosity that infects her. Desire for she knows not what. By the time she realizes it will be too late. Comings back from the brink are ever common. Yet for her, this mistake will mean the end, though a new beginning. Edenic this place, the fruit I offer means its inevitable dissolution. Lovely girl. Her tears almost already flavor my morning. Briefly. And yet even so I know that she will be stronger. I will have made her so. The sweetness she betrays will become diamond, more powerful than she could ever imagine.

How I have made her soul bleed. Would I do it again if I could have realized the extent to which I would crush her in my teeth? That question is, I suppose, unanswerable. Imagine the angst accompanying this disease. To eat the one you love, or not to eat, is always the question. Giving all of oneself, becoming one, sharing all: how often does it become literal? I would never have guessed that my heart, too, would bear the fracture as infinitely as hers. And here, my muse, I immortalize your lost innocence—it stands eternal in this space.

And then I wonder: did you expect to find so much of me here? This is the record of my soul as much as hers and hers and his. Ever-after.

Though we may be two kinds, my dearest love, you are no less dear. We will again become one. The petty falsities and fears of decay that plagued each and every one before this time now seem no more substantial than the blush of first love. And then when the two do, finally, become one, there is no more fear, no more pain, no more heartache. Coffined hearts cannot beat free of their homes. How can I deny the canker living on this rose? The unripe smell that perfumes the garden? There is no need. The garden's bloom puts shame to lesser roses. Pale flesh grown ever-so-soft wobbles so delightful as to warrant no apology. Formed glorious, reflective of the illumining moon, pallid perfection glistens into its own dew-damp glow. Each bit becomes more beautiful than the last.

The potentiality of grave love is decidedly not new. Unmatched, or perfectly matched, perhaps, it persists. Lovers find each other; they are drawn imperceptibly, magnetically. Into each other's arms forever and ever. Forever the idea plagues me. It makes its way into my work irretrievably. When I wrote the Friar's speech, it weighed. Grave love is my only tale.

> Art thou a man? Thy form cries out thou art;
> Thy tears are womanish, thy wild acts denote
> The unreasonable fury of a beast.
> Unseemly woman in a seeming man!
> Or ill-beseeming beast in seeming both!
> Wilt thou slay thy lady that in thy life lives?
> Since birth and heaven and earth, all three do meet

> In thee at once; which thou at once wouldst lose.
> Fie, fie, thou shamest thy shape, thy love, thy wit,
> Which, like a usurer, abound'st in all,
> And usest none in that true use, undead,
> Which should bedeck thy shape, thy love, thy wit.
> Thy noble shape is but a form of wax
> Digressing from the valour of a man;
> Thy dear love sworn but hollow perjury,
> Killing that love which thou hast vow'd to cherish.
> —Friar, *The Tragedy of Romeo and Juliet* [III.3]

Does your self lie in the image of your face or in the character of your soul? It is not new ground to break to say, love, that your self lies in your soul, not the wax-shape of your body that will melt away with time. And so what difference is there if you are dead or alive? What difference if there is chill from your skin or warmth? You are you, and you are the one I love. Time may come and steal your body or disease may come and take us both. Yet this love will never pass away. You are my Portia and I your William. Portia, you are the one.

Yes, killing the love that one has vowed to cherish is ever on my mind. The day that I ate her face was the day that our love really began to flourish. We became one. Her flesh filled my stomach. Her body became my own. Love and death are inextricably bound. Cupid's arrows kill. So do his teeth. And yet to eat up one's love is impossible. That is shame. Yet love persists. Apocalyptic love. More of this conversation would infect my brain.

CXVI

Let me not to the marriage of two kinds
Admit impediments. Love is not love
Which alters when it alteration finds,
Or bends with the remover to remove:
O, no! it is an ever-fixed mark,
That looks on biting and isn't shaken;
It is the star to every wandering bark,
Whose worth's unknown, although his path's mistaken.
Love's not plague's fool, though rosy lips and cheeks
Within his bending sickle's compass come;

Love alters not with his brief hours and weeks,
But bears it out even to the edge of doom.
If this be error and upon me proved,
I never zombified and none have loved.

CVIII

What's in a brain, that ink may character,
What's not obvious from my true spirit?
What's new to speak, what now to register,
That may express my love, or your dear merit?
Nothing, sweet boy; but yet, like prayers divine,
Each day I must repeat the very same;
Count no old thing old: you're mine, I'm yours,
Even as when first I hallowed your fair name.
So that eternal love in love's fresh face,
Doesn't spy the marks: ever creeping rot,
And gore dangling out of your tongue's place.
Blot the memory of the fatal shot.
Hold only the first days of love in head,
While honest outward form would show us dead.

XXXI

Your chest is turgid, coffined full of hearts,
Which I by lacking have supposed dead;
And there reigns Love, and all Love's loving parts,
And all those friends which I thought buried.
How many a holy and obsequious tear
Has dear religious love stolen from my eye,
As interest of the dead, which now appear
But things removed that hidden in you lie!
You are the grave where buried love does live,
Hung with the trophies of my lovers gone,
Who all their parts of me to you did give,
That due of many now is yours alone:

Their images I loved, in you I see,
And you—from them—have all the all of me.

XXXV

No more be grieved for those whom you have turned
Roses have thorns, and silver fountains mud:
Clouds and eclipses moon and sun have stained,
And loathsome canker lives in sweetest bud.
All men make faults, and even I in this,
Authorizing your trespass with compare,
Myself corrupting, salving your amiss,
Excusing your sins more than your sins are;
For to your unaware fault I bring in sense,—
Your adverse party is your advocate,—
And against myself a lawful plea commence:
Such civil war is in my love and hate,
That I an accessary needs must be,
To that sweet thief which sourly robs from me.

XL

Take all my brains, my love, yes take them all;
What have you then more than you had before?
No love, my love, that you may true love call;
All mine was yours, before you had this more.
Then, if from my heart, you my love receive,
I cannot blame you, for my love you used;
But yet be blamed, if you yourself deceive
By willful taste what in life you refused.
I do forgive your robbery, gentle thief,
Although you steal you all my poverty:
And yet, love knows it is a greater grief
To bear love's wrong, than mouth's known injury.
Lascivious grace, in whom all ill well shows,
Kill me with bites yet we must not be foes.

XLII

That she has turned is not only my grief,
And yet it may be said I loved her dearly;
That she turned you is of my wailing chief,
A loss in love that touches me more nearly.
Loving offenders thus I will excuse you:
You must love her, because you know I love her;
And for my sake even so she abuses me,
Suffering my friend for his state to walk by her.
Since I've lost you, my loss is my love's gain,
And losing her, my friend has found that loss;
Both find each other, and I lose both twain,
And both for my sake lay on me this cross:
But here's the joy; my friend and I are one;
We've both turned! So she loves but Z alone.

XLVII

Between my eye and heart a mile has grown,
And each does good turns now to the other:
When my eye famished for your face shown,
Or heart in love with sighs himself smothers,
With my love's picture then my eye will feast,
And to the painted banquet bids my heart;
Another time my eye is my heart's guest,
And in his thoughts of love can share a part:
So, either by your picture or my love,
Yourself long turned, yet present still with me;
For you're not farther than my thoughts can move:
I've locked you in my attic, bound safely.
Yet, when I sleep, your lost face in my sight
Awakes my heart, to heart's and eye's delight.

LI

Please do, my love, excuse the slow delay
Of my bearer when from you I wander:

From where you are why should I haste away?
And 'til I return, perhaps you'll wonder
Just what reason my poor beast will then find,
When swift extremity can seem but slow?
Then should I spur, though mounted on the wind,
In winged speed no motion shall I know,
Then can no horse with my hunger keep pace;
Therefore desire, of famished greed being made,
Shall neigh—no dull flesh—in his fiery race;
But love, for love, thus shall suspect my jade,—
"Since from you going, he went willful-slow,
Towards you I'll run, and give him leave to go."

LXXI

No longer mourn for me when I am dead
Than you will hear the surly sullen bell
Give warning to the world that I am fled
From this vile place and what remains is shell:
No, if you read this line, don't fail to shoot
The mind that wrote it; as my love still burns,
That I in your sweet thoughts would be forgot,
If thinking on me then should make you turn.
O! if,—I say you look upon this verse,
While I'm wandering in unrest of day,
Do not fail to park my corpse in a hearse;
But let your love even with my life decay;
Lest the wise world should look into your moan,
And end you with me after I am gone.

LXXIII

That time of year you may in me behold
When yellow leaves, or none, or few, still hang
Upon those boughs which shake against the cold,
Bare ruined choirs, where late the sweet birds sang.

In me you see the twilight of such day
As after sunset faded in the west;
Which by and by black night displaced away,
Death's second self, that seals the blessed in rest.
In me you see the glowing of such fire,
That on the ashes of its youth will lie,
As the death-bed, whereon it must expire,
'Til fresh unnatural food brings its revive.
This you perceive, which makes your love more strong,
To love that well, which you must leave 'fore long.

CLI

Rebirth is too young to know of conscience,
Yet who knows not conscience is born of love?
Then, gentle cheater, urge not me amiss,
Lest guilty of my faults your sweet self prove:
For, you betraying me, I do betray
My nobler part to my gross body's treason;
My soul must tell my body that he may
Triumph in love; flesh stays no farther reason:
Rising at your motion still seeks to dance,
With his triumphant prize. Proud of this pride,
He is contented with sweet necromance,
Standing in your affairs, swelling inside.
It's no want of conscience that I still call
Her "love," for whose dear love I rise and fall.

CXLVIII

O me! what eyes has Love put in my head,
Which have no correspondence with true sight;
Or, if they have, where is my judgment fled,
That censures falsely what they see aright?
If that is fair whereon my false eyes dote,
What means the world to say it is not so?

If it is not, then love must well denote
Love's eye is not so true as all men's: no,
How can it? O! how can Love's eye be true,
When mourning ends with turning not with tears?
No marvel then, though I mistake my view;
The sun itself sees not, till heaven clears.
O cunning Love! with tears you keep me blind,
Lest eyes well-seeing your foul faults should find.

CL

O! what's given you this powerful might,
With immovable weight my heart to sway?
To make me tell the lie to my true sight,
And swear that brightness does not grace the day?
How have you this magic despite vile ill
That in the very refuse of your deeds
Abides in strength, mitigating my will,
Such that, in my mind, your worst best exceeds?
Who taught you how to make me love you more,
The more I hear and see just cause of hate?
O! though I love what others do abhor,
With others you should not abhor my state:
If your unworthiness raised love in me,
More worthy I, your beloved zombie.

13

The Cure

Can you, when you have push'd out your gates the very defender of them, and in a violent popular ignorance given your enemy your shield, think to front his revenges with the easy groans of old women, the virginal palms of your daughters, or with the palsied intercession of such a decay'd dotant as you seem to be? Can you think to blow out the intended fire your city is ready to flame in with such weak breath as this? No, you are deceiv'd; therefore back to Rome and prepare for your execution. You are condemn'd; our general has sworn you out of reprieve and pardon.—First Watch, *The Tragedy of Coriolanus* (V.2)

Must we live condemned? Is there no pardon for the disease that plagues the earth?

Oh! Would that I could return the decay that withers my moments into turgid, verdant life! There is no condemnation more severe than that which I myself heap on my head. For I would live were it possible and never would I extinguish the breath of another. Yet I am torn. Again.

To be or not to be, I ask myself. There is no doubt that without brains, without flesh and organs, I would cease to be. Without turning others, our kind would eventually dissipate from the earth. There is likewise no doubt that without my kind there would be no hope for humanity. There is no reason for them to suffer any longer. I offer to the world hope.

The question is not whether or not there is a cure for this disease, but whether the cure is rather the turning of humanity than the purge of the zombie plague. There is so much in the everyday world that deserves eradication. Lady Macbeth! Out, spot. Your hands are stained so much darker than my mouth. Purging the vile from the heart of humanity is surely a good; perhaps it is the only virtue to be sought. The heart of the zombie is always pure. This is the end of the plague, the endgame of the zombie nation. Nothing short of complete zombification can save the best of the world. There is nothing impure about our hearts now. We are simple, our motivations are clear. There is no veneer of falsity that covers our pursuits. Implacably honest, to the very one, we seek to feed. We tell it like it is. We are the cure for a diseased human race. The disease of a disease can be no other than a cure. One disease destroys the other. Health returns.

And yet I am torn as readily as my willing prey. There is ever hope springing eternal that there might someday be an elixir of health. Perhaps apothecaries will compound just the right medicine bringing this horror to its end.

Any zombie cure must start with death and resurrection. This is the Christian model. There are at least five instances of resurrection in the Christian Bible: Jesus raises a widow's son in Luke 7, Jairus' daughter in Matthew 9, Lazarus in John 11, and of course Jesus himself raises in Matthew 28. We mustn't forget Samuel's spirit (who is summoned by the witch of Endor) in 1 Samuel 28. It is of central importance biblically that those returned to life retain the essential self. How can we be surprised that there is as much self in this resurrection as in any of the others?

Most obviously, we do not fear death. Not the first death, having been resurrected, nor the second death, for irreplaceable singularity—that I am special and singular, one amongst the many—is already exposed as myth. Each member of the horde is no longer irreplaceable. We are fundamentally replaceable. There is no more singularity. There is only life for the hive. No will can withstand the call to join nor can any will outman the rest. Now and now alone, in this time that is unique in all human history, have greed, lust, sloth, wrath, envy, and pride been curtailed. There is no more need for lust; it is satisfied. Sloth is immediately cured by the onset of the disease. All are driven to feed. Greed is buried as all seek the same end together; nothing short of universal conversion can satisfy. And what could possibly anger any of us? Whatever masquerades as anger is merely instinctive self-preservation. None with more than the rest can be envied as the place of each is fixed and immotile. There is likewise no more need for or basis of pride. What I was once is no longer.

What of gluttony, you ask? Gluttony itself is the means for the cure. It is the all-consuming drive that unites us to overcome our human limitation.

Yet even so, hope remains. There is hope in the real possibility of the cure. This is no mere tautology, no Ouroboros. It is in hope that the cure can exist, and it is only in the hope that the cure can exist. It is also only in the cure that hope can exist. For though we persisted previously, there was no hope that this system would improve: unless we fed it. There was no real possibility that we might become what we are not, that we might become someone who matters. I was among the most important men in England and I was as impotent as the rest. Until I was cured.

Some days I think the hope for the cure lies in remembering my children. It comes in finding the joys of their days and in watching them grow into whole beings in and out of the wreckage. It comes from imparting and preserving wisdom. It comes when bastard Miranda with her doe eyes asks after her father's story and I give it, grounding her in and over the world. We all want to know from whence we've come; it is among the only clues toward where we will go. That knowledge sustains us in the chaos. The cure is in self-knowledge and the courage to stay true, Laertes.

Other days the cure is brains. Pure and simple and gray. Brains. Brains. Brains...

XXXIII

Many glorious mornings had I seen
Flatter the mountain tops with sovereign eye,
Kissing with golden face the meadows green,
Gilding pale streams with heavenly alchemy;
He, calm, permits the basest clouds to ride
In ugly track on his celestial face,
And from the forlorn world his visage hides,
Stealing unseen to west with this disgrace:
Even so my sun one early morn hot shone,
With all triumphant splendor on my brow;
But then, Oh! The plague rained down unknown,
The radiation cloud masking 'til now
Bright Earth's sun; yet my love will not disdain
Hope for recovery despite plague's dark stain.

XXXIV

Why did you promise such a beautiful day,
And make me travel without my kevlar,

To let base crowds overtake me in my way,
Hiding your bravery from their rotten scars?
It's not enough that through the dust you break,
To dry the tears on my storm-beaten face,
For no man well of such a salve can speak,
That heals the wound, and cures not the disgrace:
Nor can your shame cure my soul's deepest grief;
Though you repent, yet I have still the loss:
The offender's sorrow lends but weak relief
To him that bears the strong offence's cross.
Ah! But hear the shrieks from your love who bleeds,
Share my riches! It ransoms your ill deeds.

CLIII

Two people walk into a bar: one short
Round guy with wings and one sick gorgeous blonde;
He falls asleep drunk, so another girl
Strips him, steals his mojo, and leaves him unmanned.
The thief-girl makes a cure from his mojo
For the impotence afflicting zombies;
Wouldn't you be all kinds of angry, too?
It is the worst part of apocalypse.
So I tried the mojo cure, best-hoping
That it would fix all my sagging manhood.
Nothing save that could redeem my moping.
Sadly, it failed. Angry, flaccid, I fled—
Groaning wild, hungry for my mistress' eyes...
Malady's only cure in her body lies.

CLIV

The little Love-god lying once asleep,
Laid by his side his heart-inflaming brand,
While many nymphs that vowed chaste life to keep
Came tripping by; but in her maiden hand

The fairest votary took up that fire
Which many legions of true hearts had warmed;
And so the general of hot desire
Was, sleeping, by a virgin hand disarmed.
This brand she quenched in a well, cool and pure
Which from Love's fire took heat perpetual,
Drawing a bath and the one zombie cure,
For men diseased; but I, my mistress' thrall,
Came there for cure and this by that I prove,
Disease pollutes water, water cools not love.

CXX

That you were once unkind befriends me now,
And for that sorrow, which I then did feel,
Needs must I under my transgression bow,
Unless my brains were bashed or shot with steel.
For if you were by my unkindness shaken,
As I by yours, you've passed a hell of time;
And I, a convert, have no leisure taken
To weigh how once I suffered in your crime.
O! that at night I might have remembered
My deepest sense, how hard true sorrow hits,
And soon to you, as you to me, then tendered
The humble salve, which bitten bosoms fits!
Like me become, your self becomes the fee;
Mine ransoms yours, and yours must ransom me.

LXXII

O! lest the world should task you to recite
What merit lived in me, that you should love
After my death,—dear love, forget me quite:
I am unworthy of cure from above;
Unless you would devise some virtuous lie,
To do more for me than mine own dessert,

And hang more praise upon deceased I
Than stingy truth would willingly impart:
O! lest your true love may seem false in this
That you for love speak well of me untrue,
My name be buried though my body's not,
And live no more to shame nor me nor you.
With worthless jaws I will in shame go forth,
But you must not, to love things nothing worth.

LXXVI

Why is my verse so barren of new pride,
So far from variation or cure's change?
Why with the time do I not glance aside
To new-found methods, and to compounds strange?
Why write I still all one, ever the same,
And keep invention in a noted weed,
That every word will almost tell my name,
Showing their birth, and where they did proceed?
O! know sweet love I always write of you,
And you and love are still my argument;
I will forever gild old words to new,
With alchemy clothe my brain's deceased tent:
For as the sun is daily new and old,
So is my love still telling what is told.

LXXXII

I grant you are not pallid yet my Muse,
And therefore may without taint overlook
The dedicated words most writers use
Of their fair subject, blessing every book.
You are as fair a walker as one who,
Finding your worth no limit by my praise,
Seek serendipitously redeemed hue
By some fresher cure for time-bettering days.
Then do so, love; yet when they have devised,

What soft strained touches medicine can lend,
You, truly fair, were truly sympathized
In true plain words, by your true-telling friend;
And their gross painting might be better used
Where cheeks need blood; in you it is abused.

CXI

O! for my sake do you accuse Fortune,
The guilty goddess of my harmful deeds,
That did not better my life apportion
Than public means which public manners breeds.
Thence comes it that my name receives a brand,
And almost thence my nature is subdued
To what it feeds on, like the dyer's hand:
Pity me, then, and wish I were renewed;
Whilst, like a willing patient, I will drink,
Antibiotics to cure infection;
No bitterness that I will bitter think,
Nor double penance, to correct correction.
Pity me then, dear friend, and I assure you
Even that your pity will make me new.

CXII

Your love and pity are what's needed still,
Though vulgar disease stamps upon my brow;
For what care I who calls me well or ill,
If you overlook my bad, my good allow?
You are my all-the-world, and I must strive
To know my shames and praises from your tongue;
None else hear me, nor I to none alive,
Can speak or listen to thoughtless words flung
On my steeled senses or hurled from along.
And so profound abysm I throw all care
Of others' voices, that my zombie senses
To critic and to flatterer stopped are.

Look how with my neglect I do dispense:
You are so strongly in my purpose bred,
That all the world besides I think are dead.

CXXXIX

O! call not me to justify the wrong
That your unkindness lays upon my heart;
Wound me just with your eye, not with your tongue:
Save power for power, and slay me just in part.
Tell me you love eating flesh; in my sight,
Dear heart, forbear to glance your eye aside:
What need you wound with biting, when your might
Is more than my over pressed defense can bide?
Let me excuse you: ah! my love well knows
Her hungry looks have been mine enemies;
And therefore to my face she turns her woes,
That she elsewhere might dart her injuries:
Yet do not so; and since I am near slain,
Kill me outright with bite, and cure my pain.

CXLI

In faith I do not love you with my eyes,
For they in you a thousand errors note;
But it's my heart that loves what they despise,
On whom, despite the view, it's pleased to dote.
Nor are my ears with your tongue's tune delighted;
Nor tender feeling, to base touches prone,
Nor taste, nor smell, desire to be invited
To any cannibal feast with you alone:
But my five wits nor my five senses can
Dissuade one foolish heart from serving you.
I live unswayed the likeness of a man,
Your proud heart's slave and vassal wretch too true.
Only this plague thus far I count my gain,
That it which makes me sin conceals my stain.

14

Falling Apart

Brains. Everywhere. It is harder to focus every day. Memory will fade. Will fades.

> I look upon those pitiful concretions of lime and clay which spring up in mildewed forwardness out of the kneaded fields about our capital—upon those thin, tottering, foundationless shells... alike without difference and without fellowship, as solitary as similar—not merely with the careless disgust of an offended eye, not merely with sorrow for a desecrated landscape, but with a painful foreboding that the roots of our national greatness must be deeply cankered.—John Ruskin, "The Seven Lamps of Architecture"

Given the choice between pleasure unbounded and decaying earthly weeds, which of us would choose the latter? There is pleasure in the chaos of the apocalypse. Pleasure beyond measure. We choose to extend ourselves beyond the rooted confines of our dominion.

From *The Book of Common Prayer:*

> Forasmuch as it hath pleased Almighty God of his great mercy to take unto himself the soul of our dear brother here departed, we therefore commit his body to the ground; earth to earth, ashes to ashes, dust to dust; in sure and certain hope of the resurrection to eternal life through our Lord Jesus Christ; who shall change the body of our low estate that it may be like unto his glorious body, according to the mighty working, whereby he is able to subdue all things to himself.

Dust to dust. There is a reason that *The Book of Common Prayer* allows a focus on the body. The earliest beginnings of the epidemic were already upon us in the 1540s. It mattered what happened to the body. Sure enough, there was no mention in the bible of what exactly we might make of the furtherance of the body beyond the grave. It was to be remade. It was not to persist in stasis, rambling the earth post-funeral. And what of the shambling body? What when the minister may not say any such thing about the body of the departed? Dust that animates demands a rewriting of the service, rewritten itself to account for the distinct choice to end the tenure of the earthen vessel.

The rankest compound of villainous smell that ever offended nostril stinks from you. As it does from me. As the days pass the flesh melts from our appendages, bit by bit, hastening the hour of our eventual end. We are together in this if nothing else. There is softness in the vulnerability of our mutual bodies. There is humanity in this shared progress. Yes, humanity. In this, if not in visage, if in nothing else, we remain what we were.

What causes a zombie to break down? The passage of time, surely. Time's twin, decay, is the bane of all things undead. Though we would be effectively eternal, in practice there is no such endless existence. Even the foulest return to the earth eventually. There is beauty in falling apart, too. Rot and decay beautify the world perfectly through their very imperfection. Not for a moment would we imagine ourselves perfect.

So, though every bit of me may fall from this frame eventually, does it ever stop? I. Simply I. And what shall we make of the world falling apart? What do we do when the world falls apart? When what you have known and loved for the entire length of your memory begins to decay and rot—what then? When the face of the deep begins to rot over the ocean of memory and the tide ceases to flow, then. Then you notice, subtly at first and raucously next that the world's infection is, in fact, your own. You have given your children all that you can and nevertheless they see the world through polluted eyes. The work that has maintained everyday has become naught. The world collapses back on itself, a black hole engulfing the colors of memory.

By day a canker grows on my left hand. It started small, a colony of bacteria. A fungus perhaps. What would have been a quick-healing scab in days long since has become instead a source of ever-widening putrefaction. When the pallid knuckle began to expose from under its stretched house, smoothly gleaming white behind rotten hide, writing became ever so much more difficult. Holding the page without smearing with flesh ink is virtually impossible. Recognizing that one is becoming a shell is more frightening than any death. The bliss of the grave calls to me. My mildewed body totters toward collapse knowing that even as a pile of rubbish-bones and soupy innards there will be no rest. Rest in peace is not for the likes of the forever-decaying.

This collection could never be complete without this final paean; this must be the space for a long-delayed ode to guts. The guts. The bone cage. From within the innermost self, the storeroom of the humors, emanates the essence of each being. The innards stuff the belly even as they best fill the hungry horde: to bursting. How empty stomachs used to growl! Veritable jungles issued forth before a meal. No such audible marker of appetite persists; empty abdomens now spew their own viscera—burst forth in blatant effort to speckle the living with noxious venom. Digestion is equally impossible. Starvation extends to every body, from tummy to grandfather's swollen belly, emptiness is the only ever-present goad toward feeding. Eating entails now some complex process of entrails and emptying far too complex for any but apothecaries. And they are all among the horde now, among the first to succumb. Eat we must, starve we do, vital we remain, even in undeath.

Human nature falls apart. That loss smarts most awfully. Whatever lies and callousness were before, whatever hurts and betrayals, whatever desires, all dissipate. While guts persist, premiere, nature's demise inversely correlates.

When I fear anything at all, I fear Shakespeare. I fear that within me lives the responsibility for this awful plague. I didn't create it, but I am as guilty of continuing it as I am of portraying it covertly onstage. I glorify violence and repugnance as I find them by giving them a home. My tribute is paid with eyes. Yet for some reason the hand of God stays the eye of heaven from too-hot burning my very soul. The blowing wind fails to consume me with its fury. Even fire is not my destroyer. Yet. So while I have license yet to persist, I tell my story in all its rotting grace. And the fear dissipates as fast as the hunger pains when fresh meat hits the entrails.

Perhaps these will be my last words. Mmmm. They are delicious.

LXXIX

While I alone could call upon your aid,
My verse alone had all your gentle grace;
But now my gracious numbers are decayed,
And my sick Muse must grace another place.

I grant, sweet love, your lovely argument
Deserves the travail of a worthier pen;
Yet what of you your poet might invent
He robs you of, and pays it you again.
He lends you virtue, and he stole that word
From your behavior; beauty he may give,
And found it in your cheek: he can afford
No praise, but what already in you lived.
Then don't thank him for that which he may say,
And please don't bite; count words not flesh as pay.

LXXX

O! how I faint when I of your soul write,
Knowing a frightful spirit's taken your name,
And in terror thereof spends all his might,
To have out my tongue speaking of your fame!
But since your worth—wide as the ocean was,
The humble as the proudest sail can bear,
My saucy bark, inferior far to his,
On your broad bay may willfully appear.
Your shallowest nod will hold me up afloat,
While I from your soundless progress still hide;
Or, being wrecked, I am a worthless boat,
Shambling along while he still keeps good pride:
Then if he thrive and I be cast away,
The worst was this: my love was my decay.

CXVIII

Like appetizers make appetites keen,
And palate cleansers prepare the next course,
So, to prevent harsh maladies unseen,
We sicken to taste dead, spoiled, unfresh corpse.
Thus, full of your never-cloying sweetness,
With bitter sauces did I frame my feeding;

And, sick of wellness, found a vast weakness
For the diseased, desperately needing
Savory parts, though I anticipate
Every ill that pains me for sin assured.
Though brought by medicine to healthful state
Which, absent goodness would by ill be cured;
I find unfortunate the lesson true,
Drugs poison him that so fell sick of you.

CXIX

What potions have I drunk of Siren tears,
Distilled from bodies foul as hell within,
Applying fears to hopes, and hopes to fears,
Still losing when I saw myself to win!
What wretched errors has my heart committed,
Whilst it hath thought itself so blessed never!
How have mine eyes out of their spheres been fitted,
In the distraction of this madding fever!
O benefit of ill! now I find true
That better is, by evil still made better;
And ruined love, when it is built anew,
Grows fairer than at first, more strong, far greater.
So I return rebuked from my ferment,
And gain by ill thrice more than I have spent.

CXXI

It's better to be vile than vile esteemed,
When not to be receives reproach of living;
And the just pleasure lost, which is so deemed
Not by our feeling, but by others' seeing:
For why should others' false adulterate eyes
Give salutation to my draining blood?
Or on my frailties why are frailer spies,
Which in their wills count bad what I think good?

No, I am that I am, and they that level
At my abuses reckon up their own:
I may be dead though they themselves be devils;
By their rank thoughts, my deeds cannot be shown;
Unless this general evil they maintain,
All men are bad and in their badness reign.

CXXIII

No, plague, you shall never boast that I change:
Your body piles built up with newer might
To me are nothing novel, nothing strange;
They are but dressings of a former sight.
Our dates are brief, and therefore we admire
What you would foist upon us that is old;
And rather make them born to our desire
Than think that we before have heard them told.
Your contagion and you I both defy,
Eschewing the present, ignoring past,
For your records and what we see tell lies,
Made more or less by your continual taste.
This I do vow and this shall ever be;
I will be true despite your scythe and me.

CXXXII

Your eyes I love, yet, still pitying me,
Betray your heart, torment me with disdain;
They've put on black, and loving mourners be,
Looking with pretty grief upon my pain.
And truly not the morning sun of heaven
Better becomes the grey cheeks of the east,
Nor that full star that ushers in the evening,
Does half that glory to the sober west,
As those two mourning eyes become your gray face:
O! let it then as well beseem your part

To mourn for me since mourning does you grace,
And suits pity despite your captive heart.
Then will I swear beauty herself is black,
And all those foul who your complexion lack.

XCV

How sugared and lovely you make the shame
Which, like a canker in the fragrant rose,
Spots the beauty of your green budding name!
O! in what sweets do you your sins enclose.
That tongue that tells the story of your days,
Making lascivious groans on your sport,
Cannot dispraise, but in a kind of praise;
Naming your name, blesses an ill report.
On what mansion did those vices alight
Which for their cottage chose your swift body,
Where beauty's veil might cover every bite
And all things turn to fair that eyes can see!
Take heed, dear heart, of this fake news story:
Best sounding words cover the most gory.

XCVIII

From you have I been absent in the spring,
When proud-pied April, dressed in all his trim,
Has put a spirit of youth in everything,
That heavy Saturn laughed and leaped with him.
Yet not the songs of birds, nor the sweet smell
Of different flowers in odor and in hue,
Could make me any summer's story tell,
Or from their proud lap pluck them where they grew:
Nor did I wonder at the lily's white,
Nor praise the deep vermillion in the rose;
They were but sweet, but figures of delight,
Drawn after you, you pattern of all those.

Yet seems it winter still, and you away,
As from your grave all these sprung forth to play.

CII

My love is strengthened, though more weak in seeming;
I love not less, though less the show appear;
That love is merchandised, whose rich esteeming,
The owner's tongue does publish everywhere.
Our love was new, and then but in the spring,
When I was wont to greet it with my lays;
As Philomel in summer's front does sing,
And stops her pipe in growth of riper days:
Not that the summer is less pleasant now
Than when her mournful hymns quite hushed the night,
But that wild music burdens every bough,
And sweets grown common lose their dear delight.
Therefore, like her, I must now hold my tongue:
Because it's fallen out, your praise unsung.

CVI

When in the chronicle of wasted time
I see descriptions of the fairest ones,
And beauty making beautiful old rime,
In praise of ladies dead and lovely sons,
Then, in the blazon of sweet beauty's best,
Of hand, of foot, of lip, of eye, of brow,
I see their antique pen would have expressed
Such grotesque beauty as you master now.
So all their praises are but prophecies
Of this our time, all you prefiguring;
And before they looked but with living eyes,
They had not skill enough your worth to sing:
For we, who now behold these present days,
Have mouths to hunger, but lack tongues to praise.

CXLVII

My love does have a fever longing still,
For that which longer nurses the disease;
Feeding on that which still preserves the ill,
The uncertain sickly appetite to please.
My reason, the physician to my love,
Angry that his prescriptions are not kept,
Has left me, and I, desperate, now approve
The desire for death, which medicine failed.
Past cure I am, now Reason is past care,
And frantic-mad with evermore unrest;
My thoughts and my discourse as madmen's are,
At random from the truth vainly expressed;
For I have sworn you fair, and thought you bright,
Who are swelled bubonic, as dark as night.

Index